# INSANITY 5
# WONDER

BY *CAMERON JACE*

www.CameronJace.com

First Original Edition, December 2015
Copyright ©2015 Cameron Jace

D0028001

Special thanks to
Greetje Wijnstok, Hannah Flood, Laura Guilbault & Sadie Muncy
– among others – for their dedication, friendship, & keen
insights with the tiniest details of the story.

How to read this book:

Begin at the beginning
and go until you come to the end;
then wait for the next book.

For those who believe they're neither their past or future,
but this very moment.
The now.

# Prologue Part One

## *BIG BEN, LONDON*

Mr. Tick and Mrs. Tock were dangling their feet, sipping tea and eating brownies on top of the Big Ben tower in London. Mr. Tick was tall, lanky, with a head that looked like a cantaloupe. He wore a long coat, but short enough at the bottom that his rainbow-colored socks showed from underneath. He didn't wear boots, but sandals, which gave way to his big toes. Mr. Tick had three hairies on top of his head. He spent a significant time nourishing and combing them. He wondered whether to comb them to the left, to the right, or spike them up with gel. Maybe going freestyle was the next move.

But Mr. Tick's most precious item was the golden watch that dangled from his pocket. A watch that Mrs. Tock liked to made fun of.

"You're on time, Mr. Tick," she said. "Just like you've always been."

"I'm not on time, Mrs. Tock," Mr. Tick said. "It's you who is always late, Mrs. Tock."

"That's my job. I have no choice," she said, leaning on her cane, the back of her short, stocky figure arching forward. "The Tick always arrives first, then the Tock follows. The rules of time since the beginning of time."

"Complaining much?" Mr. Tick's chin turned up and away from her. He was staring at the city of London buried in heavy rain, drinking raindrops from a teacup in his hand. "Blame it on the Gods of Wonderland. They're who made us that way."

"Sexist Gods," Mrs. Tock said. "Why do women always come second in their calculations? I'd prefer to be a Tick, not a Tock. I'd have loved to always arrive sooner, not later."

"Too late for that," Mr. Tick mocked her. "Look at you. You're old, short, stocky, and can barely walk with ease. I think being Mrs. Tock suits you fine."

"Yeah?" She sneered, her white hair flapping to a breeze. "And you're tall. Too tall. Bald. And thin. The characteristics of a loon."

"We're all loons in Wonderland," he said, amusing himself. "Besides, I'm not bald. I have three hairies."

This comeback irritated Mrs. Tock. So she hit him in the knees with her cane. Mr. Tick's skinny frame collapsed to his knees. Immediately, she plucked out one of his hairies.

"Ouch," he said.

"Ouch, indeed." She sneered again. "Now you only have two. Bother me further, and I'll cut off your head like the Queen of Hearts does."

"You can't do that to me, vicious woman." He slowly stood up, snatching the hairy back from her hand. He spat on it then plastered it back on his head. "I'm Mr. Tick. I work for Time itself. I can't die."

"Not if I kill you first. And you know what's good about being Mrs. Tock? I'll die after you, since I always come second." She stuck out her tongue. "Which will give me the pleasure of watching you take your last breath."

"All right." He waved his watch in the air. "Just bloody calm down. Go play with one of your cards to kill time, lazy woman."

"And you go sip your tasteless six o'clock tea like you do every day, monotonous man."

"I hate you so much now." He sighed. "You used to be fun when we were in Wonderland."

"That's because Wonderland was fun, enough that I overlooked your shortcomings, you tall and stupid Mr. Tick."

"Ah, those days may never come back." He sighed again. "Remember when were allowed to stop time?"

Now she glowered. "Oh, my. That was frabjous. I remember how we messed with the Hatter's mind when every hour stayed six o'clock for six years, and he would go mad trying to change it."

"I do. I do." He chuckled. "I really miss those days. I wonder if the Real Alice will ever show up so we can go back to Wonderland."

"I wonder." Now she sighed, hugging his tall frame by the waist.

Emotions surged through Mr. Tick's soul. He stared at the Big Ben. The famous clock was a few seconds late. Mr Tick cursed the human inaccuracy. "Look at what those humans did to Big Ben, Mrs. Tock."

"I know, Mr. Tick. Horrible. Even I don't arrive that late."

"Tell you what." Mr. Tick gripped her by the shoulders and lifted her up to look in her eyes. "How about we play, like in the old days."

"What do you mean?"

His eyes veered sideways toward Big Ben. "Let's stop time again!"

"Really? In this world?"

"Absolutely. Let's drive people mad."

"A very mimsy idea, Mr. Tick. I was starting to get bored out of my mind."

Mr. Tick put her back down then pulled out his pocket watch, fiddling with its hands. "Clock. Clock. Clock. Tick. Tac. Tock." He started humming.

So did Mrs. Tock.

Slowly they watched London freeze into a dull and grey portrait of people, traffic, and amazing architecture caught under inanimate drops of rain, now hanging in midair.

Mr. Tick and Mrs. Tock couldn't be happier. No one had the power to do this but them. After all, they were working for Mr Time himself, and they had been unhappily married since the beginning of... well... time itself.

# Prologue Part Two

### STREETS OF LONDON

Now that the time on Big Ben had frozen at six o'clock, Mr. Tick and Mrs. Tock descended to the streets. It was so much fun with everyone stuck in their place and position.

A man talking on the phone, his mouth left agape.

A woman strolling a shopping cart, still bent over it, one leg up behind her.

A speeding car stopped with an aura of its shadow stretching behind it, like in Road Runner cartoon.

"What now, Mrs. Tock?"

"I'm enjoying this. Look at those people frozen, unaware of what's happening to them. Do you want to slap a few people on the face?"

"Not fun enough."

"Empty their pockets and leave them broke when they wake up?"

"Still not fun enough."

"You could lift me up so I poke their noses."

"Seriously?"

"Oh," Mrs. Tock said. "I think I know what you will consider fun enough." She smirked.

"You nasty little short Tock." His eyes widened. "You always know how to please me."

Mrs. Tock's cheeks reddened. She shrugged her shoulders and walked the streets. The first thing she did was push a car near the edge of the bridge, so when they brought time back the driver would have no time to veer it back, and would splash into the River Thames.

Mr. Tick caught the idea and started manipulating people's positions. Now two strangers, man and woman, were kissing. Another two, one slapped the other. Then there was this businessman — Mr. Tick took his clothes off. Now he'd wake up naked in public.

On and on, they spent the next few minutes preparing the world for chaos. They even pulled a couple of news reporters from their desks and placed them ready with their microphones and cameras on the streets, so the news would go viral on the spot.

"Oh, fantastic!" Mrs. Tock knocked her cane on the ground.

"I can't wait to watch what happens," Mr. Tick said, fiddling with his time-stopping watch again. "Ready?"

"So eager to see the world in chaos."

But right before Mr. Tick could bring back time, his phone buzzed. An old banana cell phone that hadn't beeped since about fifteen years ago — who'd call time, anyways?

"Someone's calling me?" Mr. Tick said.

"It's a message," Mrs. Tock corrected him. "Why haven't I received one too?"

Then her phone buzzed.

"You're Mrs. Tock. You're always late, that's why." Mr. Tick glanced at his phone and read the message. Mrs. Tock struggled with opening hers, as she wasn't tech savvy.

"What does it say?" she asked.

"It's an offer," Mr. Tick said. "Someone knows we're bored to death."

"What kind of offer?"

"An offer from a Wonderland Monster." Mr. Tick's eyes met hers.

"Oh." She considered this. "Well, we love chaos, but we're not quite Wonderland Monsters."

"That's what I've been thinking. We don't belong to either Black Chess or the Inklings. I think we should decline the offer."

"But what's it about?"

"It's an offer to hurt someone." Mr. Tick shrugged. "Really hurt someone."

"Why would a Wonderland Monster think we'd accept that?"

"Because we're bored. And honestly, as time, we're known to be cruel."

"That's it?"

"And because it's about Alice."

"Alice?"

"Yes, Alice."

"Alice who?"

"Alice. Alice."

"The Real Alice?"

"Just Alice."

"Did they find her?"

"Not sure yet, but they think we're supposed to do something to her to confirm she is the Real Alice."

"Alice is dead."

"That's not what the message says."

"Hmm..." Mrs. Tock said. "Wouldn't it be frabjous if Alice is alive. What else does the message say?"

Mr. Tick neared Mrs. Tock and whispered in her ear. Mrs. Tock's eyes bulged. She almost lost balance with her cane. "Really?"

"I think we should do it," Mr. Tick said. "I'm curious – and very, very bored."

"Of course we should do it." She sneered all of a sudden. "I never thought so much fun was possible. But first..."

"I know," Mr. Tick said, rubbing his watch. "Let's first bring back time and watch this beautiful chaos in the streets of London."

# Chapter 1

## *LECTURE HALL, OXFORD UNIVERSITY*

Hi, my name is Alice. Could be Mary Ann. Who knows? What matters is that I am a person who saves lives. I really exist.

So I am sitting in a Physics 202 class in Oxford University, trying to learn. Having gotten permission from Dr. Tom Truckle to attend classes, I've been coming to college for the last two weeks. If I've learned anything about studying in college, it'd be that learning sucks.

The professor is talking gibberish about the scientific possibility of time traveling. He mentions Einstein a couple of times. I am about to raise a hand and tell him about the Einstein Blackboard in Oxford University, the one I used to travel back to Wonderland.

But who'd believe me if I told the story? Better keep it to myself.

The Real Alice from Wonderland is now a lame student in college, taking the road usually taken by every young boy and girl in the world. Grow up, study, get your certificates, get married, have kids, and die. Thank you very much for attending the joke called life.

They end up not knowing about the Wonderland Monsters trying to bring this world down every week — although it's been two weeks now and no monster showed up.

I think I have grown a measure of pessimism lately. How can't I when I am sitting all alone in a long row in the auditorium? All by myself. It's been the same since the first day I arrived.

Students don't talk to me here. Someone spread the news about the girl who killed her classmates in a school bus a few years ago. That mad girl, you know her? Stay away from her. She is bad news.

At least they don't know I live in an asylum.

And here I am. The professor speaks. The students listen. I am the lonely black sheep trying to fit in this world.

On a few occasions I want to scream at them and tell them how I saved their assess every week. But I'm a mad girl, after all. Everything I say is laughable, even if it's the sanest thing in the world.

Somehow, in all this mess, all I think about now is Jack. Wouldn't it be fun if he were here with me?

But Jack is gone. I have no idea why. Since two weeks ago when I traveled to Mushroomland, he hasn't shown up. I feel guilty leaving him behind in the asylum, and hope to God nothing bad has happened to him.

The lecture ends and I get out.

I take the walk of shame into the hall, eyes stuck on me, whispers behind my back, and a blurry future in front of me.

Future? The word resonates because I wonder how it's possible to think of my future when I hardly know enough about my past.

Who am I? Mary Ann? Alice? The Real Alice? An orphan? Who are my real parents? Is any of this really happening?

Still walking, I come across a peculiar picture framed on the university's walls. A photo of one of its most memorable professors. Professor Carter Pillar.

Funny how he looks like a nerd in the photo — a few years back, I suppose. The photo must have been taken before he read the Alice's Adventures Under Ground books. Before he went mad and killed twelve people.

Am I ever going to see you again, Pillar?

Last time I saw him he told me he'd see me in fourteen years. I know he looked like he meant it. As he is sometimes a vicious and morally conflicted man, it's hard to confess this: I miss him.

Fourteen years is a long time, professor. I've been thinking about it for the last two weeks. And I wonder: does it have anything to do with the number written on my cell wall? January 14th?

I walk through the Tom Quad and leave the university. Outside, people are gathered. The streets are in chaos. Car accidents everywhere. A man has drowned in the river, they say.

Everyone is bothered, concerned, and worried. All but me. Because it looks like a Wonderland Monster has arrived.

Is it a bad thing to admit I'm happy? Oh, how bored I have been without a Wonderland Monster in the picture.

# Chapter 2

## THE INKLINGS BAR, OXFORD

Back in the Inklings, I am thinking there is a new mission for me. But I am wrong.

Fabiola, once the White Queen and the Vatican's most loved woman, is sitting by a table near a bar, drinking beer. She is surrounded with all sorts of drunk customers who have more tattoos than hers. It's a drinking contest. Fabiola is winning. I can't believe my eyes.

Fabiola gulps. A man gulps. Man falls unconscious to the table, and all Fabiola says is "Next!" Then she burps and wipes her mouth with the back of her hand.

"Hey, Alice," she says on my way in. "Want in?"

I don't even answer her. I roll my eyes and move on to the March Hare.

The genius professor is cleaning the floor, talking to himself in whispers. I think he is thinking in equations, or of a new design for a garden. He still thinks Black Chess installed the light bulb in his head. Maybe he is right. Sometimes I wonder: don't we all have light bulbs in our heads?

The March is also surrounded by a few of the children we saved in Columbia. They follow him everywhere, but he refuses to give up his broom.

"He is like a child." I wink at the children. "You need to ask him politely."

They laugh at me and say, "He is a child, Alice."

"March," I say. "How have you been?"

"Better than Fabiola." He nods toward her, but she doesn't hear him.

"Yeah," I say. "What's with the drinking contest?"

"She is upset."

"Why?"

"A little earlier, a few women who knew her from the Vatican came all the way here asking for confessions and advice."

"Oh. What happened then?"

"She told them, 'If you want to ask Him something, just raise your hands and say it.' Then she offered them a beer. One of the women left crying. Another said Fabiola was possessed by the devil. This one before them, isn't the White Queen anymore."

"I see."

"And then someone came and asked for the Pillar."

"I suppose this didn't end well at all."

"She threw a glass at him and threw him out."

"I wonder why she hates him so much," I say.

"I wonder if she can ever forget her days in Wonderland."

"So you know how Fabiola was before becoming a nun?"

The conversation is interrupted by Fabiola. "It's time to start real Inklings work."

"I was hoping you'd tell me a new Wonderland Monster arrived," I say.

She wipes her mouth again, looking a bit tipsy. "Worse."

"Really?" the March says.

"Is this about the chaos on the streets of London?" I say.

"The chaos is only a handshake with darkness." Fabiola kicks a man out of his chair and tells him to leave, then pulls the chair over and sits. "Sit down. This new mission is different."

I sit. "A scarier Wonderland Monster?"

"That's too soon to tell. What we have here is an offer."

"An offer? From whom?"

"From the most vicious killer in history," Fabiola says. "A murderer. He always arrives in time. Not a tick too soon, and not a tock too late."

# Chapter 3

There isn't much time to digest the sentence Fabiola uttered. The bar's door flings open. A man and a woman enter. Everyone else leaves immediately.

The man is tall and has an oval head. Like a cantaloupe. The woman is stocky, short, and mean. There is something wicked about them. Not exactly morbid. But a feeling of inevitability surges through me. Then I realize who they are. Time itself.

"You think she is the one, Mrs. Tock?" the tall man asks the short woman, as if I am a silent picture on the wall.

"Could be." Mrs. Tock knocks her cane on the floor. "Hard to tell. But she's got that look."

"What look exactly?" Mr. Tick says.

"The look that says, 'I can't go back to yesterday because blah blah blah.'"

I find myself staring at my tattoo.

"Meet Mr. Tick and Mrs. Tock," Fabiola says, obviously not fond of them. "The two creeps that messed up time in Wonderland."

"Pleasure to meet you again, White Queen." Mr. Tick plays with his hairies. "Sad to see you go from warrior to drunk, though."

Fabiola grips the chair tighter, but suppresses her anger.

"How does it feel to deceive people into thinking you're an angel in the Vatican?" Mrs. Tock says. "Or, tell you what, let's skip the subject for now. We're here for the girl."

"Me?" I say.

"Didn't Fabiola tell you about the offer?" Mr. Tick says.

"She was about to."

"Let me summarize it for you." He grabs a seat and sits, tapping his pocket watch. "I'm afraid we have little time."

"But you're time." March Hare says.

"Shut up, March," Mrs. Tock says. "Go play with kids. Or eat your cereal."

I'm about to stand up for him when Fabiola grips my hand. I sit back, reluctant to know what's going on.

"We have an offer from Black Chess," Mr. Tick says.

"So we're playing with open cards now?" Fabiola says.

"Why not? The Inklings are ready. So is Black Chess. All in the name of World War Wonderland."

"Get to the point," I demand. "Who in Black Chess sent you?"

"The big guys, which I'm not going to reveal," Mr. Tick says. "Trust me. My offer is more tempting than knowing who really runs Black Chess."

"I'm listening," I say.

"She is feisty, Mr. Tick," Mrs. Tock remarks.

"A desirable trait if she really is her," Mr. Tick says.

"Cut the crap," I say. "Why are you here? Talk or leave."

"Before we talk, let me ask you a question," Mr. Tick says, leaning forward. "What do you know about time travel?"

# Chapter 4

"That's it." I stand up. "You better leave now."

"Wait, Alice." Fabiola pulls me back again. "Time travel is real. Not like the Einstein Blackboard, which only sends you back to Wonderland."

I sit down.

"Only Mr. Tick and I," Mrs. Tock says, "can execute time travel."

"Although there are a few conditions that have to present themselves to properly do it," Mr. Tick says. "But you don't need to worry about that."

"Why do I need to worry about it in the first place?"

"Because of our offer," Mrs. Tock says. "We want to make you time travel."

"What kind of offer is that?" I say.

"We want to send you to the future," Mr. Tick says.

"Is this a joke?"

"We're time, darling," Mrs. Tock says. "We don't joke."

"Ask older people," Mr. Tick adds. "Or the man who just missed his ride outside."

"Or the student who's going to fail tomorrow's test because he didn't respect us, time, enough and ended up sleeping through his classes," Mrs. Tock says.

"Or the man who is going to die in" — Mr. Tick stares at his watch — "about three seconds before he ever did what he always wanted to do."

"And why?" Mrs. Tock snickers at Mr. Tick.

"Because he thought that time, us, is on his side." Mr. Tick high-fives Mrs. Tock. He has to lower his hands though.

"We get it," Fabiola says. "Tell us why you want to send Alice to the future. Why would Black Chess openly offer us this? What's the point?"

"Didn't you figure it out yet?" Mrs. Tock sneers.

"Here is the deal," Mr. Tick says. "Black Chess will use our services because we have common business interests. They want to send Alice into the future so she can locate what's left of the Six Impossible Keys."

# Chapter 5

"Wouldn't it be more convenient to send me back in time to know where I hid them?" I ask.

"And risk the possibility that you may have changed their location in the past twelve years and then forgot about it?" Mr. Tick says.

"Or better, the possibility of you using them for your own cause while you're in the past?" Mrs. Tock says.

"I'm not sure I'm following," I say.

"The logic is that in the future, the keys should have been already used, and that either Black Chess or the Inklings has already won the Wonderland Wars," Mr. Tick says. "Also, there is one other advantage."

"Which is?"

"The rules of time are that you can bring objects back from the future, but not from the past to the future," Mr. Tick says.

"Aren't you time? Change the rules," I say.

"We're actually working for Time. Mr. Time doesn't want to be known at this time in history. But we have full authority to talk on his behalf," Mr. Tick says. "So just humor us. We can't send you into the future without your consent."

"So let's say she follows this loony plan and brings back the keys from the future," Fabiola says. "Why would Black Chess help us do that?"

"Black Chess's problem is the whereabouts of the Six Impossible Keys. Taking them by force from you isn't the trouble. They believe they are stronger," Mr. Tick says. "So the idea is bring the keys, have them in your possession, and fight us when we try to take them from you. They're up to that challenge."

If I accept, we'll have to have a plan to hide the keys immediately. Maybe I can find a way to send a message back to the future. It's risky.

"What do you think, Fabiola?" I say.

"I say no. Because you're the only one who knows the whereabouts of the keys. Sooner or later, you'll find them here without their help. They need us. We don't need them."

"Wouldn't you want to know for sure if you're the Real Alice?" Mr. Tick asks me. "Think of it. All the evidence you gathered from the past could have been given to you. Maybe the sneaky Pillar played you into thinking you were the Real Alice. How do you know he didn't plant the keys you found in the basement of your house and made you think you'd found them yourself?"

"I met Lewis Carroll's ghost in here," I say. "He told me I'm the Real Alice."

"It's a ghost. An apparition. Who said it can't be manipulated?" Mr. Tick argues. "But the future never lies. You will definitely know if you're the Real Alice by finding all the keys there and knowing what happens to you in the future."

"I'm not so keen about my future without my past," I say. "I think I'll decline. Please leave now."

"She leaves us no choice, Mrs. Tock," Mr. Tick tells his wife.

"I hate it when people don't accept our kindness." Mrs. Tock shakes her head.

Suddenly the March Hare stiffens in place, as if electrified by an invisible current. He falls to the floor.

"We planted this. Cyanide in his milk," Mr. Tick says. "To wake him up, he needs an antidote. And only we have it."

Fabiola reaches for her Vorpal sword, but neither of the two loons flinch.

"I wouldn't do that, because the only way to save the March Hare is to go back in time and relieve him from his poison," Mrs. Tock sneers, all the joy in the world flaming in her eyes. "Cyanide is incurable."

"Besides, it's time that cuts like a knife. Not a Vorpal sword," Mr. Tick mocks Fabiola. "So please sit down and accept our offer."

I stare at their ugly faces without flinching. I muster the look of the unafraid, but my knees are shaking. Not the March Hare. Please don't kill him.

"Think of it as a school trip on a bus," Mr. Tick tells me. "Except you don't have to kill your classmates this time."

"You'll also get to know Jack's fate in the future," Mr. Tick says. "I think you want to know about that.

"Shut up, you creeps." I grit my teeth. "Let's do it. Send me to the future."

# Chapter 6

Margaret Kent had her acquaintances gathered around her. The Cheshire, Carolus Ludovicus, and a crew of Red mercenaries. She sat back in her chair, imagining she would be Queen when this was all over. It was simple, really. She would get the keys, chop off the Queen of Hearts' head, and play football with it in a festive celebration broadcast on live TV.

But it was a long road to freedom.

"Mr. Tick and Mrs. Tock offered Alice the deal, and she took the bait," Margaret said. "It's only hours and the Six Impossible Keys will be ours."

"Meow." The Cheshire moaned happily, still disguised in Jack's body, which made him look weirder.

"Don't meow in my office." Margaret groaned. "This is Parliament, not a barn."

Carolus laughed next to the Cheshire. He had just gotten his Lullaby shot, a sedative that kept him calm enough not to kill anyone, or to look for Lewis Carroll to kill him.

Margaret actually felt nauseated, having a man looking like Lewis Carroll and another looking like Jack Diamonds in her office. It seemed so wrong, but she didn't want to give it much thought now.

"My point is that sending Alice into the future is taking place at the Inklings," she said. "It's your job to surround the place, and make sure to get the keys by force when she wakes up."

"What if she tries to trick us?" Carolus asked.

"Then you bring her to me. We'll torture her until she tells us where the keys are."

"Could I volunteer to do the torture?" the Cheshire said. "I'd like to see the look on her face, being tortured by Jack, the love of her life."

Margaret smirked. "Nasty idea. Brilliant."

"We've always been two messed-up individuals," the Cheshire said.

"Me too," Carolus said eagerly.

"One happy family." Margaret rolled her eyes. "Wait and see how much we'll want to kill each other when we find the keys."

"Meow." That was Carolus this time.

Margaret glared at him.

"You said you don't want the Cheshire to meow, not me," Carolus said.

"Your meow sucks," the Cheshire said.

"Yeah?" Carolus said, and stared him in the eyes.

"Yeah," the Cheshire retorted. "It lacks cat subtlety."

"What the hell is that?"

"Something only cats can do," the Cheshire said.

"Like grinning?" Carolus grinned, mustering a Lewis Carroll look. Which really irritated Margaret.

"Your grinning would scare only a child," the Cheshire argued. "Mine makes a soldier piss in his boots."

"You mean a cat piss in his boots. Want to punch me in the face to show me how to grin and meow? Ha!" Carolus began to lose his temper.

"Seriously," the Cheshire said. "You're nothing without a pill thinking it's a man. You're a ghost of a man at best."

"Girls!" Margaret rapped her hand on the desk.

"He started it." Carolus grunted.

"What?" The Cheshire rolled his eyes. "Is this high school on mushrooms all over again?"

"You never went to school," Margaret shouted. "Stop it, and let's talk about the Inklings."

"What about it?" the Cheshire said.

"I heard rumors it has a secret tunnel you can use to escape," Margaret said. "So go make sure Alice won't escape when she wakes up."

"Will do," Carolus said.

"Aren't you coming?" the Cheshire asked Margaret.

"No." She sat back in her comfortable leather chair, tonguing a pen in her mouth. "I have to tell the Queen about my plan with the keys."

"She doesn't know yet?" Carolus said.

"Not yet, and there is a reason for it." Margaret smirked.

# Chapter 7

## *SOMEWHERE IN THE FUTURE*

I wake up in a big bed inside a white room with cushiony drapes and modern furniture. I am suffering from a headache. Mr. Tick and Mrs. Tock told me it would subside soon. It's surreal to imagine another version of me lying on a couch a few years ago in the back room in the Inklings, while I am here in the future. All at the same time.

I straighten up, remembering that the March Hare's life is at stake. I haven't had enough time to get to know him, but he reminds of Constance, whom I saved in my first mission. Both are pure children at heart, and all I want to do is hold them tight and protect them.

But where am I? How many years into the future? And how has the Inklings turned into this beautiful room I am in?

The headache begins to subside and I get off the bed. This room is big and beautiful. Mostly white.

I am wearing a white dress. The tiles on the floor are black and white, like a chessboard. Except they're made of elegant, expensive, shiny material, like I have never seen before.

There is a window to my right, overlooking a garden. It catches my eye. I can't help but go look.

The garden is vast. Endless. Full of lilies and greens. It reminds me of... wait... is that a hedgehog of a rabbit?

It is.

No. Not a rabbit. A March Hare.

I realize the garden is another fabulous replica of Wonderland, probably designed by the March Hare — in the future.

Does this mean he is alive? Does this mean I will succeed in getting back the keys and saving him?

Too many ideas roam in my head and stir that headache back again. It's surreal being in the future. All those possibilities.

I turn and face the room again.

I walk to a wardrobe — probably *my* wardrobe. When I open it, my mouth hangs open. Look at those beautiful shoes. And at those endless, beautiful dresses. All mine? I pick one after the other and take a better look at them. They don't look my size. A little bigger, belong someone who is a bit chubby.

Then it occurs to me. I am in the future. I could have gained weight. How old am I?

I put down the dresses and locate the mirror in the room. A wall mirror. Beautiful as well, with calligraphy on the white frame.

Standing there and staring at my reflection, I look much different. Not just older. I have gained weight. Not much, but it explains the dresses. God, I have a couple of wrinkles under my eyes. I must be in my early thirties.

I can't tell whether this is fun or shocking, seeing myself so many years into the future. So I let it go.

"But wait, Alice," I say to my reflection. "You live in what looks like a good house. You're probably rich. Does this mean...?"

The words are stuck in my mouth. But I think all of this means that the Inklings won. There can't be another explanation. Whatever the Wonderland Wars are, I'm sure I wouldn't be living as luxuriously in the future.

Unless we won.

"We won!" I raise my hands in the air and shout like a kid with a trophy. "Yeah!" I bend my elbow and wave it in the air, as if I am surrounded by an audience of millions.

Really? We won?

I run back to the window and open it. Why isn't there a soul outside?

"We won!" I scream out at the garden. "Suck on this, Black Chess." I jab my finger at no one.

I am jumping in my room. Left and right. Wondering where my friends are. What happened to them in the future? Fabiola. The March Hare. The Pillar. Where are they?

And Jack? Is it possible I found a way for Jack to stay in this world?

All kinds of thoughts weigh down on my shoulders. I can hardly breathe from the excitement. I need to meet someone to get answers.

I run to the door, hoping to meet whoever is living with me in the house.

But then I stop. My heart drops to the floor when I hear a voice outside. It's not a voice of a Wonderland Monster.

It's a sweet voice.

Of a child.

But it scares the heck out of me.

Why?

Because there is a little girl, standing by the door. She is about six years old. She has blond hair, flabby cheeks, and an incredibly amazing smile. She is holding a lollipop. Licking it.

She looks at me.

Then she says, "What's taking you so long, Mum?"

# Chapter 8

Margaret stood before the Queen, watching her feed peanuts to her dogs. The Queen awarded them one each, only after they slobbered and licked her feet. The Queen liked the feeling while she drank bone broth of the people whose heads she had chopped off last week. Human bone broth gave her power, like drinking an enemy's blood from their skulls.

"Brilliant plan, Margaret," the Queen said. "I thought you were dumb. But you turned out to be a little better than that. Rather stupid, which is way better than dumb."

"Thank you, My Queen." Margaret wasn't going to comment. Like always, she sucked in all the humiliation until she got what she wanted. "But that's not just it."

"What could you have possibly done better than getting the keys from Alice by sending her to the future?"

"The fact that only I control the aspects of this plan, My Queen."

The Queen stopped feeding her dogs. She spat out the bone broth at them. The poor pets moaned and lowered their chins to the floor. "What do you mean, Margaret?"

"I mean the keys will be delivered to me, not you, My Queen." Margaret tried not to snicker or smile. When doing business, a poker face was her mask.

"I'm not sure I heard you well."

"No, you did," Margaret said, hands laced before her. "And I'm not going to repeat myself."

"Holy Lords of Wonderland." The Queen sighed. "Are you blackmailing me?"

"Who said I'm blackmailing you, My Majesty?"

"You said the keys will be delivered only to you, and not to me."

"That's right, but it doesn't mean I will not deliver them to you."

"I'm paradoxically, nonsensically, unexplainably confused."

*Because you are dumb little thing.* "Why so, My Queen? I will deliver you the keys, under one condition."

"You *are* blackmailing me."

"I wouldn't call it that. Think of it as a small employee in a large company asking for a raise in exchange for the things they do and never take credit for."

"It's still blackmail." The Queen chewed on a nut. "So you want a raise?"

*I want to be the queen, but it's too soon to bring that to the table.* "No. I don't want a raise."

"It's Mary Go Round all over again. You're blackmailing me, but you're not blackmailing me. You want a raise but you don't want a raise. A puzzle?"

"Not at all." Margaret took a single step forward. "I will give you the keys if you give me what I want."

"Which is?"

"You know what I want."

The Queen dropped her nut. She finally got it.

"I want what you have taken from me." Margaret's eyes moistened, although she'd sworn to hold back her emotions. "I want what made me become your tool for so many years. It's time you bring it back."

"You know I don't want to give that back to you." The Queen stared at her from top to bottom.

"But it's mine. Not yours."

"I believe things are only yours if you have them." The Queen smiled flatly. "How can they be yours if you don't?"

"They were mine once."

"But they aren't now. See the logic?"

"Then you get no keys." Margaret collected herself and took a step back. "And you know what I can do with them."

"I don't think you know what the keys are for, Margaret," the Queen said. "And you know I can chop your head off right now." She glanced at her bowl of bone broth on the table. "How I'd love to drink your brain in that bowl."

"Suit yourself." Margaret turned and walked to the door.

"Wait." Margaret didn't turn and face the Queen so she'd keep up the tension. "I will give you what you want, but you must know you will be my enemy then."

"I understand."

"I hurt my enemies bad, Margaret."

"I've witnessed that."

"As you wish," the Queen chirped. "What's wrong with getting the keys in exchange for this stupid thing you want from me?" she mumbled. "Bring me the keys. You get what you want."

"Thank you," Margaret said, and walked out to the hallway, her chin up. She mustered her Duchess face as she dealt with all kinds of businesses.

A few moments later, she took the elevator, waited until she was alone, and began crying her heart out.

# Chapter 9

## SOMEWHERE IN THE FUTURE

I am standing clueless in the most surreal situation you can imagine, trapped in my future self, and staring at my future daughter. Oh my God, I just noticed her hair's texture is a replica of mine. And her walk reminds of myself. I'm going to cry bubblegum tears right now.

"Mummy, we're late," she says. "Have you slept in again?"

I kneel to the floor and open my arms, wanting her to jump into them. Instead, she stares at me, as if I am a loon. Then I realize I don't even know her name.

"What's wrong with you, Mummy?" she says. "Did you take your pills?"

"Pills? Huh," I say, not caring about pills. "How about you come into Mummy's arms?"

"Ooofff." She stomps her feet and blows out a long sigh, showing her bubbly cheeks. "All right."

She approaches me, and my heartbeat is like a freight train. Then she slowly throws herself into my arms. I squeeze her so tight. I can't help it. Tears squeeze out of my eyes. This feels so good. So illegally good.

"Mummy, you're choking me," she says. "What's wrong with you today?" She slides herself away and stares into my eyes. "Do you want me to tell Dad to drive me to school?"

"Dad?" I raise an eyebrow. Is it Jack? Really? It must be Jack. She has those light dimples in her cheeks. It must be Jack.

Then another voice calls from the hallway. Not that of an adult. Another kid. A boy.

"Lily!" the boy calls. "Where are you? I need to go."

"Lily?" I stare at my daughter.

"Yes, Lily, Mum. It's not like I chose the name."

"Lily is a nice name," I say. I love it, actually.

"Yeah, so you say." She rolls her eyes. "At least it's a better than Tiger." She points at the boy, a little older, standing by the door.

"Tiger?" I stare at him.

"Yes, Tiger," she mumbles. "Hey, Tiger. Come meet Mum."

"Thanks, I've seen her before." Tiger giggles.

"Because she acts like she hasn't seen us before."

"Then she didn't take her meds," Tiger says.

I am at a loss for words, staring at my cute kids and experiencing something I've never thought of before. Hell, I haven't even experienced being married. And frankly, I thought a girl who was out there to save the world wasn't going to fall in love and have kids, ever.

But wait. Tiger and Lily? Is that why my plant in my cell means so much to me? Does this mean I have been into the future before?

"She is in a daze," Tiger says. "Let's get Dad to drive us to school."

"No." I stand up. "I will drive you to school." It's my responsibility, isn't it? "Have you had breakfast yet?"

Both stare at me as if I am an alien.

"Did I say something wrong?" I say.

"You never make us breakfast," Lily says.

"Oh." I rub my chin. "That was a bad mum. Not from now on."

Tiger and Lily burst out laughing.

"Dad won't believe this." Lily says.

And then Dad calls. He sounds like he is down in the foyer or something. My room is on the second floor. And he says, "Baby, are you awake yet?"

Suddenly, and upon hearing his voice, I realize I don't want to see him.

# Chapter 10

The man calling me *baby* isn't Jack. That's not his voice. I've never heard it before. No, I can't meet him. That's like a big spoiler for the movie of my life. I don't want to know the man I am going to marry. I don't mind my children. They are the blood that runs in my veins. I don't mind meeting them now. But not the boy who will become a man I will fall in love with. I will have a boring love life this way when I get back.

"Listen." I kneel down. "How about we make it a surprise to Dad, the fact that I am making you breakfast? Let's not see him now."

"What do you want us to do?" Tiger says.

"Let's leave through the back stairs. Get into my car. I have a car, right?"

"If you call your fancy rabbit-looking vehicle a car." Tiger rolls his eyes.

"Okay." I nod. "I will drive you to school, buy breakfast on the way, and then I'll come back and meet Dad. Then I will cook you the best dinner you can gorge on when you come back."

"I want marshmallow tarts," Lily says.

"I can do that." I have no idea what that is.

"Laughing Jelly Sticks, too?" Lily adds.

"Of course."

"You're the best, Mum." She hugs me again.

"You want something special, Tiger?" I say.

"I just want to see you cook, for real," he says. "That'd make my day."

"Awesome."

"Awesome?" Tiger squints, as if he's starting to suspect I'm not his mother. "Who says awesome anymore?"

"What should I say?"

"Frabjous," Lily squeaks.

"Ah." I forgot we won the Wonderland War. "Frabjous. Now any idea how we could sneak out without Dad seeing us?"

"You're the boss, Mum," he says. "That's your problem."

"Of course," I say, unsure what my next move will be.

There is a man who calls me baby climbing up the stairs. My eyes veer toward the window again. Then to the bedsheets. Then back to my children. "How about we climb out the window?"

"Wow!" Tiger says. "You're seriously the coolest mum in the Great Republic of Wonderland."

# Chapter 11

I roll the sheets into a rope and dangle it down the window. Lily climbs on my back and wraps her tiny arms around my neck. Tiger holds me from the front, head on my bosom, arms wrapped around my back. We climb down, and I am surprised at my athletic physique. I must have trained well throughout the war. Chubby but strong.

Midway, the rope starts waving left and right, like a pendulum.

"Like Tarzan!" Tiger chirps.

"No, like Rapunzel," Lily insists.

"Like the worst mother ever," I say.

Finally, we hit the ground. My husband's voice is calling for me upstairs. He must be in my room now. And soon he'll see the dangling rope.

I let my children guide me to my car. It's around the corner from the fabulous garden. I still can't believe I'm living luxuriously in this future. Did someone compensate me that well for killing monsters and saving lives?

Tiger points at what looks like a vehicle, draped in a large white cover. It's parked in a garage full of pink roses, covered with a pergola of green leaves.

Surreal.

I uncover it, and there is one funny-looking car underneath it. It looks like a modified Corvette, redesigned into the shape of a rabbit. The front is the rabbit's nose, mouth, and chin, stretched out to serve as a car, a convertible with custom-made backseats. The back is the rabbit's ass.

"Is this my car?"

"Come on, Mum." Lily pulls me by the hand. "We've wanted you to take us for a ride in it since forever."

"Okay." I shake my shoulders. "Jump in."

They do. I get into the driver's seat. There are no keys. There is a button that says 'Push Me.'

I push and the car stirs into existence. My kids cheer behind me, ready for a ride.

"Mrs. Alice!"

I hear someone call me. Not my husband. Another voice. Familiar.

"It's Mr. Jittery. Our neighbor!" Lily says. "He designed the garden."

I turn and watch the March Hare stepping toward me. He is in his pajamas, and wears a nightcap on his head. He looks much older now.

The kids greet him and play with him for a moment. This is the first of my friends that I've seen in this fabulous future. I have so many questions for him.

"Good morning, Mrs. Alice," the March Hare says.

"Mrs. Alice?" I squint.

He dismisses my inquiry and hands me an envelope. "I thought I'd give you this back."

I take the envelope. It has pictures of six keys on a chain on the back. It doesn't look like there are keys inside.

"Thank you." I lean forward and whisper, "So we won the war?"

The March's ears stand erect. His eyes widen. It's the same look he had when I first met him in the asylum called the Hole.

"What is it? Aren't you happy?" I say. "We won the Wonderland War."

The March's face turns red. His eyes roll sideways and upward.

I pull him closer to me. "Don't tell me you still have the light bulb in your head?"

"What light bulb?" He manages a weird smile that I can't interpret.

"Come on, Mum." Lily taps me on the shoulder. "We're late for school."

I realize children come first, and decide I will talk with the March later. "Okay. But you lead the way," I tell my children, and hit the pedal.

"Bye, Mr. Jittery!" Lily waves.

"I know the way." Tiger hugs the back of the passenger seat and begins to guide me into the fantabulous world of the future.

# Chapter 12

I push the radio button while driving in this rich and luxurious neighborhood I live in. There is a song playing on the radio. It has this line, 'the future is so bright, I gotta wear shades.'

All houses are family homes, the bright colors of rainbows. Roses are everywhere. Lily greets a few people on the way. Families and their kids in silly-looking cars like mine. Whenever someone greets me, I nod and pretend I know them.

At some point I miss Tiger's directions and detour into a left. It's a one-way road. Narrow. It looks abandoned. The more I drive into it, the more roses disappear. There is a gate at the end.

"Okay, I'm lost," I tell Tiger, but he doesn't answer me.

I look in the mirror and see him and Lily are scared out of their minds. So scared Tiger can't tell me how to turn around and get back on track.

"What's wrong?"

"You shouldn't be driving this way," Tiger says.

"Yeah, I know. I missed the turn," I say. "Can you tell me how to get back?"

"He is scared," Lily says, looking as scared. "I think you have to drive over the grass here. That'll be breaking the law, but it's the only way back."

"That's silly," I say while following her suggestion. "Why isn't there a way back?"

"Because everyone knows you don't drive near this place." Tiger tenses.

I decide not to ask them while they're scared. So I begin to entertain them by singing along with a song that I don't know on the radio. It takes some time, but finally they ease up once we're closer to their school.

"We've arrived!" Lily raises her hands as I slow down at the school's curb.

It puzzles me how my children are so happy about going to school. I don't think that's the norm. But hey, we won the war. This must be the heaven version of the future.

Tiger gives me a kiss on my cheek and jumps out of the car. He meets up with his friends, looking like the leader of the tribe. Lily hugs me dearly. She gets out slowly, looking a bit shy. The first one to greet her is at the school's door. Her teacher.

Gripping the wheel, I feel worried about my little girl. I am not sure if I should do something about it. This is the future. I am going to be back within an hour. But God, it just doesn't feel right not to know why Lily is a bit introverted.

I watch her enter the building, reminding myself of the mission I am here for. I open the envelope, which is my only clue to the whereabouts of the keys. Inside, there is nothing but a piece of paper with an address.

An address I recognize immediately. St. Aldates Street. I am supposed to go to Oxford University.

I think it's my own handwriting scribbled at the bottom. It says:

Find the Mock Turtle. He knows where the keys are.

So the way to the Six Keys is to go to Oxford University and find the Mock Turtle. Not the soup, of course.

I remember a brief appearance for such a character by that name in Lewis Carroll's books. He is the one who actually tells Alice he called his teacher tortoise because he 'taught us.'

I turn around, aiming to find my way to Oxford University. I wonder if it looks as fluffy and wonderful as my neighborhood.

As I drive, I keep thinking about the note. It escapes me how and why I'd have written this note in the future. Did I know I was coming? Did I come here before, and left myself a clue?

Time traveling is even more mind-boggling than the secrets of Wonderland.

Lost in the neighborhood, I decide to make it back to the March Hare and have a lengthy conversation with him. That'd be the right start.

I come across that scary street again. And being me, I can't help it. I am curious.

I detour again, driving along, looking left and right. It's a dim-looking street, but not really scary. I keep driving until I reach the gate. I wonder how it opens. Maybe this is the way to the university.

I get out of the car and walk to the gate. There is a single red button on the right wall of the gate. It says: *Don't push this button.*

It seems that, even after we won the war, the nonsensical never stopped. Why is there a button if I shouldn't push it?

But I do. I am curious.

The gate opens slowly. And a timer appears on the wall. Sixty seconds. I assume it's the time the gate stays open.

Jumping back in my rabbit car, I hit the accelerator and gun it throughout the gate.

And it's only seconds before I see the horror and understand what's really happening in the future.

# Chapter 13

## *THE PRESENT: OXFORD*

The Cheshire had been roaming the street in Jack's body for some time. And boy was it fun.

First of all, Jack was young, and allowed the Cheshire to mingle with young people, which excited him. Yesterday he'd played a game of football. Gone to a movie with a few youngsters he befriended at the game.

Even better was how girls liked Jack. They always complimented him and flirted with him. They thought he was funny and easygoing, though the Cheshire hardly talked. He didn't want to expose himself as being a very old creature.

Usually, he only smirked, laughed, and used Jack's attractive facial expressions to push a conversation.

The best thing about him were his dimples, the girls said.

Thankfully, he knew enough about Jack to sustain believable short conversations when he forced to say something.

At the movies, everyone wanted to see the latest *Star Wars* movie. But the Cheshire persuaded them to go see *Puss in Boots.*

That was some experience for him.

Seeing a kick-ass cat, subtly evil, loved and cherished by the audience, made the Cheshire's day. Maybe humans weren't that bad after all — but soon he changed his mind and convinced himself that Puss in Boots must be a Wonderlander he hadn't heard of. One with expanded influence in this world. He should tell the Queen about him later.

Then he went to dinner with a girl. She kept holding his hand all night, showing him she liked him. She made him drive her home and spent a significant time at her doorstep, talking to him. At first he didn't understand, until she neared and kissed him.

"Meow." He moaned.

The girl backed off immediately, pretended she had school tomorrow and disappeared into her house.

"She's definitely not a cat person." he told himself.

Walking away, the Cheshire wondered about those strange human emotions. Holding hands, going to movies, kissing. Those humans sure knew how to enjoy themselves. They didn't spend their days hunting for a rat to feed themselves and their families. And they didn't spend much time evading imminent threats of predators, dogs, and passing cars.

Holy furs, grins, and purrs.

They didn't even have fleas sticking to the backs of their necks, driving them crazy all day and night.

And most important, each and every one of them had a place to go home to at night. It was just silly.

Suddenly, the Cheshire heard someone call behind him, "Alice!"

The Cheshire turned and saw no one. But the voice continued, "Alice. I love you."

The Cheshire's eyes rolled. Was he getting madder than he already was?

"I need to tell you why I came back for you, Alice."

*Enough*, the Cheshire thought. What was going on?

Then the headache started. He clapped his hands over his ears, but the voice persisted. He finally realized whose voice this really was.

It was Jack's. The Cheshire was listening to Jack's thoughts. About none other than Alice.

The Cheshire grinned. A big grin. It was time to listen to why Jack had really come back for Alice.

# Chapter 14

## *THE FUTURE*

The place I just left turned out to be a compound of some sorts. Safe and sound from the mad world outside.

Here in the streets, it's a circus of insanity. It's like a kindergarten for adults. People drive cars into each other and laugh at the injured passengers. Others are vandalizing every other building they come across. There are a bunch of what look like protestors gathered in the streets. They're holding signs that read: *We want our brains back.*

And that's just what I am capable of comprehending from a brief look.

I stop the car, too worried to get out, still trying to understand what's going on. Is this the real future? What about the place I came from?

I turn back and see my neighborhood behind the gate is protected by a fortress wall. Surveillance cameras everywhere. Several signs with warnings stretch across the walls. *Don't come near or you will be fried like toast.*

Farther to the left, there is a bigger sign. It says: *The Wonderland Compound.*

I remind myself that I am lying on a couch in the Inklings bar a few years back in time now. Does this mean the Inklings has been turned into this protective compound in the future?

Why?

Turning back, I stare at the mad world in chaos and realize I am staring at where Big Ben once stood. The building still has a clock, but it's not Big Ben anymore. It's a giant building, shaped like a mushroom.

I decide to drive further into the mad streets of London. It's not easy, considering the crazy people rapping on my car, demanding that I stop.

But I manage. Maneuvering left and right. A building is on fire next to me. A march of naked people with tattoos on their chests: *Government! Give back our brains!*

What happened here?

I arrive at what once was the British Parliament in Westminster Palace. It's not that anymore. It's something scary.

I slow down and stare at it, unable to believe my own eyes. But it's hard not to know what it has turned into.

A circus.

A fluttering flag before the tent reads: Ladies and gentlemen, mad and madders, come watch the freaks who call themselves sane and rational.

I halt to a stop, needing a moment to let it all sink in.

We didn't really win the war, did we? We lost it. Big time. And the Wonderland Monsters turned the circus around on humans. Now the insane watch the sane for entertainment and freak shows.

A slight look to the right and I see the Queen of Hearts' face, full profile, drawn on the vertical length of a ten-story building. The drawing makes her look taller, thinner, and not as ugly as she really is. Underneath her painting there are more words to read: *In Her Majesty's Bonkers Service!*

I let out a shriek inside my car. This is the worst future for mankind.

Another horde of protestors walk toward my car. Those are different and most nonsensical. They hold up signs that say: *We volunteer to have our heads off. All in the name of the Queen.*

They keep advancing and pointing at my car. They want me to let some of them in. I pull the roof of the car on and lock myself inside. But then they pull out their Bandersnatch guns and are about to shoot me. I put the car in reverse and hit the accelerator.

It doesn't work. An ambulance, driven by a madman, crashes into my car from behind.

I need to find a way out of this.

# Chapter 15

The Cheshire was going mad — well, at least madder than he already was.

Jack's voice in his head was killing him. At first he thought he could know why Jack came back for Alice. But the little piece of information didn't present itself. Instead, Jack turned out to be in real love with Alice, thinking about her all the time. Remembering how they met. All those late night phone calls. The walks. The talks. And the romance.

The Cheshire felt like he was going to vomit from the clichés and cheesiness. Humans pretended they were superior in their feelings toward each other.

But then the Cheshire remembered the youngsters he'd just met and gone to the movies with. Maybe he really had to give humans a chance.

At least guys like Jack.

How was it possible to really think about someone this way? How was Jack benefitting from loving a girl who'd killed him?

It drove the Cheshire mad. But he decided he had to figure it out. Starting with sorting Jack's mind out.

Like a cabinet full of curiosities, he wanted to locate Jack's memories with Alice. The memory in the bus where where she killed him and the other students.

# Chapter 16

## *The Future: London*

Running wild in the streets, chased by a horde of mad people, I glanced at what once was the Big Ben again. Not only does it look like a weird mushroom made of what looks like marshmallow bricks, but it has a cuckoo bursting out of it when the clock strikes. The cuckoo has a husky voice, shouting, "We're all mad here!" three times.

There is much more madness that surrounds me, but I try to focus on two things. My survival, and finding a way out of London to Oxford University.

Pictures of the Queen of Hearts are everywhere. A few statues too. One of them shows her chopping off a flamingo's head. The following words are carved underneath: *She finally did it!*

I take a left onto what I think will lead me to the road out of here. The madmen are right on my tail. From the signs I believe Great Britain is now called the Great Republic of Wonderland, just like Tiger told me.

And that's not all. There are maps on the walls of buildings. Maps of the empire of Wonderland. Apparently Black Chess colonized the rest of the world like the British Empire of the past. Mushrooms are Black Chess's trademark, planted in every country they set foot in, as a marker of territory.

Damn. The Queen's plan really worked.

Now I take a right, as I elbow one of my attackers hard enough to throw him back. I think I am stronger now. I wonder how.

There is a map that shows that the republic's most proud achievement: conquering Uncle Sam's land. The United Loons of Wonderland is what the US is called now. Hell, there is a picture of the Sphinx in Egypt with the Queen's head instead of a lion's.

This by far is the worst-case scenario. How did we lose the war?

A couple of my chasers manage to grab my hand and slow me down. I kick one in the crotch and slice a shard of glass though the other's neck. What the heck am I doing?

But I have no time. I keep on running before the others find me. This is insane. The world is chasing after me. I don't even know why.

And here it is. Oxford University. How did I just step out of London into Oxford this fast? I wonder if it has something to do with time traveling. Does time collapse distances this way?

But here I am, staring at... Wait.

At first I am surprised that the university buildings are left as they were. No mushroom structures or other sorts of nonsense have touched it. Then I read the sign hung atop the Tom Tower. It says: *Welcome to the Oxford Asylum for the Sane and Mundane.*

Pictures of Einstein on the outer walls, depicted as a madman with a hookah pipe and flapping white hair, say it all. There is a bubbling quote coming out of his mouth: *Time? What about time? Time is mad.*

But I'm not that surprised. It has all gotten out of hand already.

What does surprise me is that my chasers are now split in two groups. Left and right. Now I can't enter the university — I mean the asylum — surrounded by mad people in all directions.

I'm stuck with a shard of glass for a weapon, between two groups of mad folks wanting to kill me — or so I believe.

I stand in place, circling slowly, my eyes meeting theirs. They're approaching me. They're not in a rush. Why would they be? We have all the madness in the world.

What are you going to do right now, Alice? Die in the future? What does that even mean?

I realize that what really bothers me is that I am a mother now. Who is going to take care of Lily and Tiger if I die?

But I'm not even supposed to be here. Time traveling is really messing with my head.

The madmen and women approach me with grins worse than the Cheshire's. I swallow hard. What am I going to do? I guess I will have to fight them. Can I confront all of them?

I pray my None Fu skills have evolved tremendously, or I will die a mushroom in the future.

Suddenly, a huge vehicle stops nearby. A red one. Its wheels screech to a halt. It's a fire truck. Before I know it, the madmen, including me, are thrown backward by the rush of water pressure out of a fire hose.

Left and right, mad people glide and slide on the floor.

Who is doing this?

The mad people beg whoever is doing this to stop. But he keeps drowning us, and we're unable to see who he is behind a wall of moist air.

"Alice!" I hear someone call.

Who is that?

The water stops. The silhouette of a man appears.

I squint as he approaches me, shooting a couple of madmen with a rifle on the way.

And slowly, I can see.

The man wears a hat and blue suit, and white gloves. He is unbelievably dry in all this slippery wetness.

"Pillar?" I stand up, not believing what I am seeing.

He shoots another mad attacker then stares at his pocket watch. "Hmmm," he mumbles. "A bit too late."

"What?" I am not sure whether to laugh or cry now. "Late for what?"

"For an important date." He winks and pulls me by my hands. "I told you I'd see you again in fourteen years. Did you put some weight on?"

# Chapter 17

"How did you know I'd be sent to the future?" I ask the Pillar as he drags me into the fire truck.

"Missed you too, Alice," he says, climbing up into the driver's seat. "Now hop in."

I climb up, but one of those madmen grabs at my legs and tries to pull me down. I try to kick him away, having dropped my shards of glass, but he won't budge. The Pillar shoots him instantly with his rifle, as if we're in a zombie movie escaping brain eaters.

"That wasn't necessary," I say, locking myself inside. "You didn't have to kill him. He isn't evil. He is just mad."

"That's why I shot him." He pushes the accelerator, running a few other madmen over. "All of this isn't real, Alice. We're in the future."

"What's that supposed to mean?" I hold on to the dashboard.

The Pillar drives over a set of crashed cars. "The future is like a video game. Shoot the bad guys. And when it's 'game over,' rewind to the past and play it all over again." He shifts gears. "Now pick up a helmet from the back. We're going to set this place on fire."

"Set the place on fire?" I pull on a helmet. The Pillar never changes.

"We're firemen, aren't we?"

"Who said we're firemen?"

"We have a fire truck. Makes us firemen," he says, "So we're going to burn this miserable place down." He stares at the long line of gasoline he poured earlier, then throws a cigar into it. I remember that cigar. It's the one from when we were in Mushroomland. "Hang tight. I'll speed up."

"Pillar." I nudge him as the truck hits bumps on the ground. "You're overreacting. I'm not sure those mad people want to kill me."

"Of course they do. They know who you are."

"They know I am Alice? Why would they want to kill me, then?"

"Because you left the compound." He turns the wheel. "You see, the Wonderland Compound belongs to the richest of the rich. The ones who left the world to rot after Black Chess won the war and ruled the world."

"You're joking, right?"

"Black Chess, being the greedy Wonderlanders they are, spared the rich, like it always happens, and gave them immunity in exchange for their money and resources on the planet."

"Resources?" The truck bumps again. In the rearview mirror, I see the streets are in flames behind us.

"Black Chess needed to know about every conspiracy theory the humans held in the past. Where they hid Hitler's gold, who really controlled agriculture, if there's such a thing as UFOs, etcetera, etcetera. And only the rich knew about it."

"So they collaborated?"

"Yeah." He suddenly stops the truck. Had I not used my hand as a shield, my head would've bumped against the dashboard. I raise my head to see why he stopped. And now I see it. "Do me a favor and pick up that dog, Alice."

Immediately, I jump out of the truck and rush to pick it up. It's a German shepherd, but it seems to be either wounded or extremely hungry.

Back in the car, I rest the dog in the back as the Pillar takes off again. It's not wounded, so I shelter it and give it water and food the Pillar has stacked in the back.

I get back into the passenger seat. "You drive madmen over and save the dog?"

"Madmen had a choice to be either mad or sane. Hell, they had a choice to win the war or lose it. The dog didn't."

Again with the Pillar's logic. "So if what you're saying about the Wonderland Compound is true, why do I live there? Shouldn't I be one of the masses who lost the war? Why would I make a deal with Black Chess?"

Another bump in the road. "Later, Alice," the Pillar says. "Now tell me, did you receive the note in the envelope?"

"You know about that, too?"

"I've been here for a couple of days. I asked around, and killed a few people. I even blew up a bridge on the River Thames for the fun of it."

"Fun of it?"

"Like I said, we can always go back in time and correct the future. I'll send a note to Inspector Dormouse once we go back. I'll warn him of me blowing up the bridge in fourteen years. Happy? Now what's the address in the note?"

"Oxford University, which means we shouldn't have left and burned the street behind us."

"Oh." He raises an eyebrow and turns the wheel. The truck loops back a hundred and eighty degrees. "I love how I have the streets all for myself to play with."

Once we're in the right direction again, I don't let him drive further. I grip his hands on the wheel as tightly as I can. "Pillar. How the heck did you know I'd be here? What's going on?"

# Chapter 18

"Okay." He sighs, his white-gloved hands on the wheel. "Remember two weeks ago when Margaret fooled Fabiola into thinking she is her insider in the Queen's palace?"

"I do."

"When I figured it out, I found a way to listen to a meeting in Margaret's office in Parliament. I heard her talking to unknown members of Black Chess about the next step to get the keys. She proposed using Mr. Tick and Mrs. Tock to make you time-travel and locate them."

"I assume you know Mr. Tick and Mrs. Tock from Wonderland."

"They're the worst of the worst. Exceptionally mean. But you can't do anything to them. They don't die."

"Because they're time itself."

"That's right."

"Then why didn't you tell me?"

"Because they wouldn't approach you until everyone thought I was gone. I'm thinking this isn't just about the keys, but something much bigger. So I let them think I was gone, and followed you here to help you. After all, it's not a bad idea to find the keys all at once."

"I'm sure you have your own devious intention to have them, as always." I eye him. "But how did you time-travel yourself?"

"I used the Tom Tower. It was risky, but I had a secret parchment with a secret formula by Nikola Tesla — you know who that is, right? — about how to use the tower for time-traveling fourteen years into the future."

"Why fourteen years? What's with the number?"

"I never knew. I only heard Margaret telling Mr. Tick and Mrs. Tock fourteen years."

"This is so crazy." I hold my head in my hands. "Why send me into the future, not the past, to get the keys? I asked them, but they told me some gibberish I couldn't fathom."

"It doesn't matter," the Pillar says. "Nor does it matter how you left a note to remind *you* about the whereabouts of the keys. Maybe you have been into the future before. What matters is that we find the keys as soon as possible, then figure out a plan to hide then. You can't go back with the keys, or Black Chess will have them."

"Okay," I say. I like the Pillar when he is on point. "The note says I have to find the Mock Turtle in the Oxford Asylum. You know who he is?"

"Met him a couple of times in Wonderland. Don't even remember how he looked. He was pretty much no one. Can we go find him now?"

"Yes. I needed to know a few things first. God. I can't believe the university is an asylum now. And did you see Parliament turning into a circus?"

"Some things never change." He drives ahead. "Have you seen Mac Burger? It's Rat Burger now."

"Nothing surprises me now."

"All but the fact that we may need help to get into the asylum." He points ahead. I look and see the Oxford Asylum is heavily protected with Red mercenaries after the fire.

"Just drive through them with your truck," I say. "We can always fix the past later."

"Can't do it. We need to sneak into the asylum, not break into it, or we won't have enough time to find this Mock Turtle."

"How do we get inside, then?"

"I have an idea. A rather mad one." He turns the wheel to the left and guns it through the streets. "Glad to have you back in the future, Alice."

# Chapter 19

## *THE PRESENT: LONDON*

The Cheshire's head was about to explode. Not that he'd found answers to what he wanted to know about Alice. But Jack's continued thoughts, and caring, about the mad girl began to escalate to another level. A level of something the Cheshire had never experienced before. He thought humans called them emotions.

"Holy meows and paws," he mumbled, rubbing his chest. "In the name of my nine lives, what's that I'm feeling?"

Jack's thoughts weren't based on logic. No, not really. Not the way cats would calculate the speed, size, and distance of a scurrying rat. Jack's thoughts were silver linen to a warm buzz that filled the Cheshire's chest with light.

It was a good feeling, actually. A dash of anxiety, care, and total devotion to someone else other than the self. Something the Cheshire didn't think he'd experienced before.

He sat down on a bank, opposite the Inklings.

He was supposed to be ready for when Alice woke up with the keys, deceive her with Jack's looks, and take them from her, then bring them back to Margaret Kent.

But now the Cheshire doubted his capabilities. Not with Jack's fuzzy and utterly silly feelings about Alice. Those weren't the kinds of feelings of someone wanting to hurt another.

What in the name of paws and claws was that?

The thing that bothered him the most was that these were human feelings. The humans he'd hated all his life — and planned to hate for eternity.

How were they capable of this?

"Don't fall for it," he told himself. "It's just a facade made by the hypocrite humans. They use it to pretend they love one another while they don't. It's a cliché. It's cheesy; even more cheesy than Cheshire cheese itself. Jub Jub and slithy and full of rotten mushrooms."

But still he knew it wasn't really that. Because Jack was practically dead. And if not, the Cheshire had never possessed a soul that had the ability to mess with his brain.

These were Jack's true feelings about a girl he met in school a few years ago. It was so weird that the Cheshire began seeing her picture before his cat's eyes. Not the usual black and white, but very colorful this time.

The Cheshire heard his phone ring. It was Margaret. She was probably calling to ask about the progress of her plan. He picked up and said, "Jack speaking."

"What did you say?" the Duchess roared.

The Cheshire hadn't meant to say he was Jack. He realized that he was falling in love with Jack. Maybe Alice. Maybe both.

Because who the heck exuded so much emotion toward a person who'd killed them in a bus accident?

# Chapter 20

## *THE FUTURE: OXFORD*

"Where are we going?" I ask the Pillar.

"To meet someone who'll help us with sneaking into the asylum." The Pillar honks for the fun of it.

"Someone? Who? Are they going to lend us doctor uniforms?"

"That wouldn't work with the Reds at this time. They can smell the likes of me and you a mile away."

"Then who?"

"Someone who's practically our enemy."

"Why would we use an enemy to help us?"

"Because he has a gift like nobody else."

"Stop the puzzles, Pillar. Who?"

"The Cheshire."

I say nothing for a moment. I know how much the Pillar and the Cheshire hate each other. I also have no idea how the Cheshire might help.

"He's lost his mind in the future. Really lost his mind. He is homeless now. Like most cats in this life."

I glance back at the dog we saved. He's sleeping serenely after a big meal. "Homeless? The Cheshire?"

"I know it doesn't make sense. He should be Black Chess's favorite monster, after all he did for them to win the war."

"Then what happened to him?"

The Pillar stops the car near an abandoned building. "He's fallen in love."

"The Cheshire?" I laugh. "No way."

"Yes way," the Pillar says. "You didn't ask with whom."

"I don't think I want to know. First I need the fact that he fell in love to sink in," I say. "I mean how? He doesn't even have a real face. Who'd love someone with no face?"

"I didn't say he was loved back."

"Wow. That's even more surprising. Are you saying the evil Cheshire is a hapless romantic now?"

"Indeed." He jumps out of the car, pulling his cane along.

I follow him down. Apparently we're entering that abandoned building. "So who's the unlucky girl? Or is it a cat?"

"No, it's a girl," the Pillar says slowly. "And it's someone you know very well."

"Waltraud Wagner, my warden, would be a candidate."

"No, Alice. The Cheshire is in love with you."

# Chapter 21

We step into the abandoned building, passing by a few homeless people. Insane ones, the Pillar says. That's why he has his rifle with him. I follow him, awaiting an answer to my question: Why would the Cheshire be in love with me?

"It's complicated," the Pillar says, looking sideways, in case we get attacked by another group of mad people. "Let's start with him not really looking like a Cheshire at the moment."

"What's new? I wouldn't be surprised if he is possessing a priest."

"Worse." The Pillar ducks, scanning the place. "This time he is possessing someone dear to you."

"Dear to me?" I grimace. "All the people I know are Wonderlanders. I thought he can't possess Wonderlanders."

"Only if they're still alive," the Pillar says.

I stop, taking a moment to assess the possibilities. But who am I fooling? There is only one Wonderlander who's practically dead, and so dear to me. And he has been missing for some time. "Jack?" I cup my hands on my mouth.

The Pillar nods. "Try not to scream. We don't want to attract loonies."

"Jack?" I whisper, gritting my teeth.

"Lowering your voice isn't going to change my answer." He rolls his eyes. "Yes. Jack."

"But we're in the future. How long has he been possessing Jack's body?"

"Fourteen years."

"How is that possible? This means I never saw Jack again since he disappeared from the asylum."

"You got that right." He crawls on all fours, and I follow him into a tunnel.

"That's why I am not married to him." The words are tasteless on my tongue. Not that I was sure I wanted to marry Jack. The thought just occurred to me as the natural progress of events. "This is why I am married to that stranger back home."

"Exactly. Handsome man."

"I didn't meet him or see him. Couldn't bring myself to it," I say. "I freaked out when he called me 'baby.'"

"Nothing wrong with your husband calling you baby once in a while."

"Shut up." I pout, still crawling toward a scant light in the distance. "Poor Jack."

"The guy is a jinx," the Pillar says. "Killed by his girlfriend, possessed by her enemy. He was better off dead."

"Stop it, Pillar." I grunt. "Tell me what all of this has to do with the Cheshire being in love with me. You know how creepy this feels?"

"Don't you like his grin? I thought chicks always dig the grin." He stops for a second. "That sounded too American. Didn't it?"

"It did."

"I'm not really myself in the future, am I?"

"More smartass than you usually are," I say. "And how do you look young? You're not a day older than when I last saw you."

"Good genes." He winks, and then crawls on all fours again. "Smoking hookah is good for the skin."

"Spare me the cheesiness." I sigh. "Now how — "

I was going to ask about the Cheshire being in love with me again, but then it hits me. "Are you saying the Cheshire was exposed to Jack's mind and soul?"

"We've arrived." The Pillar kicks a small door open and steps out. "Try not to let the Cheshire see you before I talk to him first."

I follow him into what looks like a large hall in a sewer. Then when I stand up, I see the Cheshire. Oh my God. What happened to him?

# Chapter 22

The Cheshire is sitting on a chair in the middle of the stinking room. Water is dripping somewhere nearby. He is playing cards with a dead mad man on the opposite side of the table. I watch him lay his cards down while in Jack's body. Then he possesses the man in front of him for the next move. Then back to Jack.

"Cheshire." The Pillar approaches him with his rifle in his hand. I stay back like he told me. Seeing Jack having turned into a puppet on a cat's string is breaking my heart. I doubt there's anything I can do for him after all these years. Jack didn't even flinch for the moment when the Cheshire left his body. The boy must be really dead now.

"Pillar?" Jack — I mean the Cheshire — says. "Want to play cards?"

I think the notorious cat has really lost it.

"I see you have a partner already," the Pillar says, playing along.

"He's dumb," the Cheshire complains. "Every moves he makes, I already know."

"Oh, it's like you can read his mind." The Pillar glances back to me for a second. Then back to him. "I guess it means you're a genius."

"You think?" The Cheshire's grin is a lame, timid curve on Jack's haggard and older face. Who would have thought? "Please come play with me, Pillar."

"How about I tell you jokes?" the Pillar says. "I can make you laugh."

"Jokes don't work," the Cheshire scolds. "I've been telling myself jokes for fourteen years."

"Laughed your tail off?"

"On the contrary — I've never laughed once," the Cheshire says. "You know why?"

"Depressed being in someone else's body?"

"No, because I knew those jokes."

"Maybe the greatest joke you never admitted was yourself."

"It's true." The Cheshire lowers Jack's head. I can't believe my eyes. "I lost myself in someone who isn't me."

"Jack?"

"Yes. But you have no idea, Pillar. The things I heard in Jack's mind. The emotions. The sacrifice. It's addictive."

"Addictive enough you gave up on your quest to burn every human being alive?"

"I don't hate humans anymore." He chuckles. It sounds as if he's crying. "That's why Black Chess gave up on me. They say I betrayed them."

"Why do you love humans all of a sudden?"

"Jack."

"You said that before."

"And Alice." The Cheshire holds the Pillar's hand. Eagerly. For the first time, I see Jack's eyes sparkle like they used to in the past. "If you only know how I — I mean Jack loves her. It's mind-boggling."

"Listen, Chesh." The Pillar glances at his watch. "Since you love Alice so much now, she could use a favor. Can you do that?"

"Alice?" The Cheshire suddenly realizes I am in the room. The way he stares at me is the optimum of madness: to love the eyes looking at you, and hate the soul that occupies them.

# Chapter 23

"Alice!" The Cheshire — Jack — or whoever that is — runs to me and wraps his arms around me.

I stand stiff with a tear on the verge of rolling down my cheek. I don't know who is who. But I miss Jack so much. This body holding me smells of him. It talks like him. And I might want to kiss him like I wanted to kiss Jack.

"I missed you so much, Alice." He holds my head between my hands, Jack's eyes melting me on the inside.

"I missed you too, Jack." I hug him back.

"Don't fall for him," the Pillar says. "This isn't Jack."

"But — "

"Jack died inside the Cheshire a long time ago," the Pillar says. "The Cheshire has gone mad, overwhelmed by human emotions he can't understand."

"You know what this means?" I pull Jack closer to me. "It means Jack's love for me is so strong. Look what it has done to the devil himself."

The Pillar waves a hand, unable to persuade me.

"I've been looking for you for fourteen years," Jack tells me.

"I'm sorry I left you behind, Jack." I run my hand over his face. Oh, those dimples. How I've missed them. "I should have saved you from the Cheshire."

And it's then when the Pillar's pout makes sense.

It's then when I realize the horror I'm holding in my hands. I was only fooling myself. Who I am holding, whether I like it or not, is the Cheshire.

Jack is dead. For good.

I push the Cheshire back and step away.

"But I love you, Alice!" he says.

"Don't." I lift a hand in the air, looking away from a beautiful face I've always loved — and killed. Maybe I can fix that later in the future. I turn to face the Pillar. "Why did you bring me here? To play games with my mind?"

"Not at all," the Pillar says. "You might not know it, but I wouldn't do that to you."

"Then why are we here?"

"Because the Cheshire can help us enter Oxford Asylum."

"How so?"

A smile sweeps the Pillar's face as he looks at the Cheshire. "Tell me, Jack," he says. "Would you do anything for the one you love?"

# Chapter 24

The woman in the red fur walked into the Queen's chamber. She had her black glasses on and said nothing.

"It wasn't hard to find you," the Queen said.

"The deal was that I'd stay away," the woman said. Her words were stiff. Practical.

"True." The Queen nodded. "You did well. Although you shouldn't have been seen in Oxford University or the Wembley Stadium."

"I couldn't help watching the arrival of the Wonderland Monsters," she said. "The Cheshire's arrival to this world was epic. The watermelons stuffed with children's heads, too. Later, I kept to myself and hid, like you instructed me."

"Does that mean you know who is bringing the monsters back?"

"Not at all," the woman said. "I was only curious. Other than that, I'm just here for one mission. You know what that is."

"I know," the Queen said. "You have what I need from you, then?"

"You mean what Margaret wants?"

"Semantics," the Queen said. "I took from her what she needed; now she wants it back in exchange of a favor."

"I have it." The woman nodded. "Do you want me to hand it to you?"

"You brought it with you?"

"I'm not comfortable with calling it *it*, but yes, I have it."

"Good. I will have my guards see you to a guest room with the chubby boy," the Queen said. "Once I get what I want from Margaret, I will send for you."

"Of course, My Queen," the woman said, and turned to face the guiding guards.

"Wait," the Queen said.

"Yes?" The woman turned around

"You know what you will do when I ask for you, right?" The Queen smirked.

"Yes, I do." The woman smirked and walked away.

The Queen felt exceptionally euphoric. She jumped in place and yelled at the top of her lungs, "Guards!"

A couple of them hurried into the room.

"Off with your head!" she ordered.

The guards looked perplexed, staring at each other. "Which of our heads do you want to chop off, My Queen? Me or him?"

"Who cares." She waved a hand and sat on her throne. "I just want to see a head roll before me. Now!"

# Chapter 25

## *THE FUTURE: OXFORD ASYLUM*

I am lying on a patient's bed, rolled by a young doctor inside the asylum. The doctor is signing my admission papers, telling the nurses I'm a sane person caught outside. Turns out the Queen ordered all sane people into asylums all over the world. Sane people are fed well inside until their turn comes to attend Westminster Circus, where the mad take revenge on the sane.

Whatever all of this means.

The doctor finishes the papers and starts rolling me inside. The doctor is not really a doctor. He is the Pillar possessing a young doctor's soul.

The deal the Pillar made was to let the Cheshire help him possess another person's soul so we could figure out our way into the asylum. I didn't know it before, but the soul-possessing gift can be passed. The Cheshire never told it to anyone. He only agreed because he thinks he loves me. And the Pillar, being the Pillar, took immoral advantage of that.

"Don't move until I find a way to get to that Mock Turtle," the Pillar says in the doctor's voice. Poor, handsome doctor, blond hair, well built, under the Pillar's influence now.

"How are you going to find him?" I ask.

"The lesser-practiced art of asking, dear Alice," the Pillar says. "It works like a charm when you're good looking."

He stops by a couple of nurses. "Sweeties," I hear him say. "Looking fantastic today."

"Oh." One of them blushes — I tilt my head to see her. She is a redhead. "Thank you, doctor. What was your name again?"

Oops. We didn't ask before the Pillar possessed him.

"Call me doctor." The Pillar smiles.

"Doctor?" the other one, shorter, with thick glasses, asks.

"Of course. Dr. *Doctor*," the Pillar says. "Instead of James, Jack, or John. Boring, right?"

They giggle. "How can we help you, Dr. Doctor?"

"See how sweet the words drool out of your sugary mouth?" he says.

I close my eyes, roll them behind my eyelids, and try not to laugh.

"You're so sweet," the shorter one says.

"Did you ever hear about that patient, Mock Turtle?" the Pillar says.

"Of course," the bigger nurse says. "Pfff. The revolutionist."

"Revolutionist?"

"You don't go out much to the real world, do you?" the shorter one says. "Never heard about the Inklings?"

Things are getting weirder by the minute.

"Excuse my ignorance," the Pillar says. "But I hate those sane people already."

"The Mock Turtle is the leader of the revolution against the Queen," the bigger one says.

"Long live the Queen," the shorter one adds.

"Of course, long live the Queen," the Pillar says. "Although she's too short to live that long," he says under his breath.

I wonder about the Inklings in the future. Who is leading them in the future? And why am I in a compound, living a luxurious life away from them? Part of a plan?

"Do you know where I can find him, sweeties?" the Pillar says.

"He is in section six," the shorter one says.

"And where is that?"

"The one known as the Door to Wonderland in Christ Church. But you must have heard of it."

"Of course I have." The Pillar fluff-talks them for a few seconds and then rolls my bed ahead.

"You really know where this Door to Wonderland is?" I say, tilting my head back to look at him.

"I do. It's a door near the library that Lewis Carroll used to stare at for hours while writing the book," the Pillar says. "It's said that the dean of the university at the time locked it because it was a real door to Wonderland. And..."

"And what?"

"It's supposed to be your favorite place for playing as a child."

"Me?"

"Yes," the Pillar says. "In fact, it makes sense for this Mock Turtle to wait for you there. If you really keep the keys with him, then the name of the place is like a secret code between you and him. Your favorite childhood place. Makes sense."

"Do you think me living in the compound is a camouflage, a trick to hide my true identity in the future, and the Mock Turtle being the leader of the revolution is only to delude the Queen?"

"We're about to know in a second." The Pillar stops.

I get out of bed and stare at the door he is pointing at. It leads to a garden. A vast one that is the same design as the one in my house at the compound. It looks like another part of Wonderland.

"I'm very curious about this Mock Turtle now," I say. "Who could it be?"

"The last person that would ever cross your mind," the Pillar says, pointing at him standing in the middle of the garden.

# Chapter 26

The phone rang, and Margaret picked it up. "Who is it?"

"The Cheshire."

"What do you want?" she said. "Aren't you supposed to guard the Inklings until Alice awakes?"

"Something came up."

"What's that?"

"I'm getting signals from Jack's mind."

"Signals?"

"I can read his mind."

"You don't say."

"I'm seeing memories."

"I bet they're all playing cards and None Fu games."

"No." The Cheshire hesitated. Margaret sensed he wasn't quite himself. Something was happening to him. "They're mostly about Alice."

Margaret shrugged. She stood up, locked her door, and went back to her desk. "Anything useful?"

"A lot of lovey-dovey memories," he said. "I'm still digging."

"Anything about her being the Real Alice?" she asked eagerly. "Come on, there must a lead in her past to prove it's her."

"You sound too eager to know."

"Yes, Cheshire, I want to know." She gritted her teeth. "You know what it means if it's hers."

"Not really sure," he lamented. "I'm not that involved in this Wonderland War."

"You don't understand," Margaret said. "All of the Real Alice's secrets lay in the few years after the circus. That's where it all happened. You have to rummage through that wreckage in Jack's mind. Harder."

The Cheshire kept to himself for a while. Margaret couldn't dismiss the possibility that the infamous cat was warming up to Jack and Alice, even if just a little.

"Cheshire," she said. "What's going on?"

"Nothing." He was surely lying. "There is this memory about why Jack came back after she killed him."

"And?"

"I can't put my finger on it," the Cheshire said. "But he came back to tell her something so important to him."

"Tell her who she really is, maybe?" Margaret leaned back in her chair, a smile curving her lips. "That's fantastic."

"It's driving me crazy."

"You are crazy."

"You think so?"

"'We're all mad here.' Your words, not mine."

"Yeah. I forgot."

"It's okay. Just understand that things are starting to get really exciting."

"I don't understand."

"You don't have to. Just figure out why Jack came back, and if she is the Real Alice." Margaret hung up then closed her eyes.

The few past weeks she had resisted the idea that the Pillar had found the Real Alice. It was a scary thought to Wonderlanders. But there hadn't been enough evidence to support it.

Since Margaret needed all she could bargain with to get her thing back from the Queen, it'd be great if she came across proof that the girl in the asylum was the Real Alice. That would be perfect timing.

# Chapter 27

*THE FUTURE: THE DOOR TO WONDERLAND, OXFORD ASYLUM FOR THE CRIMINALLY SANE*

Like the Pillar said, the Mock Turtle isn't who I expected him to be. All the scenarios I imagined were out of context. Surprises keep on coming.

"Is that really him?" I ask the Pillar, pointing at the so-called Mock Turtle.

"Dr. Tom Truckle himself." The Pillar is as confused as I am.

"He is the revolution leader?" I scratch my head, as if I am in a big cartoon show called life. "And how come he is the Mock Turtle?"

"He likes mock turtle soup a lot," the Pillar remarks. "We should've noticed."

I think about it for a moment. The puzzle starts to unfold in my mind. "And there is something else that should have given him away."

"What's that?" the Pillar asks.

"Tom Truckle is an anagram for Mock Turtle."

The Pillar's eyes glimmer. "Clever. But the question is: did he know he was the Mock Turtle back then when we were in the asylum?"

"And why did I leave the secret to the keys' whereabouts with this old, annoying man?"

"Let's see." We walk toward Truckle. "Honestly, he doesn't look as tense as in the past. Little too old for leading a revolution, though."

"You shouldn't be here," Tom Truckle says, leaning against a tree in the garden. From what it looks like, this isn't just a garden. It's a prison, walled with enormous trees and stinging bushes. There is nowhere to escape. "My wardens will arrive soon. They'll know who you are."

"Do you know who I am?" the Pillar says.

"Why should I care?" Tom says. "I was talking to Alice."

I realize Tom doesn't know I'm from the past, so I need to play along while I get answers at the same time. "It's okay, Tom," I tell him. "Where are the keys?"

Tom fidgets, pulls out a few pills, swallows them dry. He looks at me. "I can't talk here," he whispers. "You have to get me out of here. How did you even get in?" He grabs me by the shoulders. "And why have you left the compound?"

"Hey," the Pillar says. "We're getting ahead of ourselves. Let's start with getting you out of here. But first, we need to make sure the keys aren't here in the asylum."

"Who are you?" Tom says.

"It doesn't matter," I tell him. "Stick with me. Are the keys inside the asylum?"

"No," Tom says.

"Then my friend is right. Let's get you out of here first."

"Tell me how, and I'm all yours," Tom says. He cranes his head over my shoulder, his mouth agape. "Oh, no."

"What's wrong?" I say.

The Pillar taps me on the shoulder, looking in the same direction behind me. There is a TV hung above the door. It shows the Great Republic of Wonderland news. I've been declared a fugitive. Public enemy number one. The Queen has ordered my head chopped off for breaking the treaty and leaving the compound.

"The deal was that strict?" I ask the Pillar.

"Like I said, rich people stay in their compound for immunity, but they're not allowed to ever leave it."

"Why would I agree to such terms?"

The Pillar shrugs. I turn to Tom, and he gives me a look that worries me. He knows something I don't know. "Show me out first," he demands.

Two wardens arrive at the door, one of them whistling a warning. Suddenly the place is head over heels.

"Alice," the Pillar says. "I have a great idea how to get out of here."

"Please tell me."

The Pillar raises an eyebrow and says, "Run!"

# Chapter 28

When the Pillar says run, you realize you're in great danger. This is what Tom Truckle does. Even the Pillar himself disappears in the flash of an eye, probably behind the bushes, because this place is actually a small prison of trees and vicious flowers.

There is nowhere out of here, except climbing over the high walls in the back or through the door we came from.

I find myself stranded, but unafraid of the Reds by the door. It's not like I haven't confronted them before. It's just never happened with my back against the wall.

"What are you doing?" Tom Truckle says from behind the bushes. "They'll kill you. You're wanted since you broke the treaty and left the compound."

What am I doing? Heck, I have no idea. Something inside urges me to fight back. I suppose this is a more experienced version of myself in the future, even with the few pounds I've put on.

One of the Reds steps forward and talks to me from the hollow darkness of his mask. "We don't have to do this, Mrs. Wonder. If you comply and let me send you back to the compound, everything will be fine."

I am about to scratch my head. Just like that, bring me back to the compound? Didn't the Queen declare me a fugitive? Is that a trick?

He extends a hand. "Please, will you come with me?"

"And my friends?"

"You have no friends in here, Mrs. Wonder," the Red says. "You're only a bit confused. Have you taken your medication today?"

Again? Tiger, my son, asked me if I had taken my pills this morning. What is that all about?

I resort to silence, readying my fist for a fight.

"Mrs. Wonder, please don't," the Red says.

"I'm not leaving without my friends. Either you let us go, or else."

"I can't let you go. Queen's orders. But I can spare you from having your head chopped off and send you back to the compound." Why do I have a feeling he also fears me?

"No, I will not comply," I say.

The Reds behind him gather and begin to approach me. First the nines, then the eights, the sevens, and so on. There's about thirty of them in this small garden in Christ Church. I wonder why the Pillar lets me fight alone. I know he can choke them with his hookah.

The first two Reds run toward me. I find myself curving my body and slightly maneuvering to one side. The two slash the air with their swords, but one hurts the other.

Well, that was neat. Where did I learn that?

"Reds!" the leader roars, and four others approach, grunting behind their cloaks. It's time for a real fight.

# Chapter 29

This time, and I still don't know how I am doing this, I run to the nearest tree, and with speed I find myself walk perpendicularly on its surface for a second. Then I somersault back in the air. Just as if I am professional parkour runner, tapping on the edges of walls and trees and walking on thin wires.

Wow. That feels good.

Instead of landing back on the ground, I land on their heads. Amazingly, I tap on each Red's head quickly, breaking them, but never falling to the ground. Then finally, when they're nothing but empty cloaks crumbled on the grass, I land on my feet. Like a ballerina.

"Huh." I rub imaginary dust from my clothes. "Not bad for a thirty-three-year-old mum."

"You think you can outsmart all of us?" the leader says. "With that silly None Fu of yours?"

Oh, so that's it. None Fu in the future. Pretty dope.

"Reds!"

Now it's ten of them. They're carrying swords. I don't carry one because I am swift, agile, and can almost walk on air.

I raise my hands in the air, as if I were the Karate Kid. Tension fills the air. They can't predict my next move. I give in to my inner future powers and let my body do what feels right. This time I am running in their direction. I duck the first sword. Pull the cloak from under a Red. When he disappears, and I have the cloak for myself, I use it against the slashing sword of another Red. The cloak is incredibly uncuttable — a bit elastic, though. I wrap it around the Red's sword until I force him to let go of it. I catch the sword in midair with one hand while I choke him with the cloak.

I am *so* having fun.

Too stubborn to use the sword, I throw it up in the air and, like a mad ballerina, kick the Reds left and right while binding their cloaks into one another. I'm basically like a hurricane in a cartoon movie, swirling through them, and there is nothing they can do about it.

I end up with a bunch of Red cloaks that I can make a good, long rope from.

Standing erect, I finally face the leader of the Reds, now standing alone, pretending he isn't afraid of me.

"You think we will spare you, Mrs. Wonder?" he says. "More Reds are on their way."

"That's sad," I say. "Because you will not have enough time to give them orders."

The Reds leader seems confused by my confidence. I raise my head and look for the sword I'd thrown up in the sky. Now it comes down, slashing him in two symmetrical halves.

Someone claps behind me, applauding my performance. I swirl back to face my next enemy, but it's only the Pillar, sitting on a chair, smoking a hookah in the middle of the garden. Now back in real Pillar form. No more possessing doctors.

"You abandoned me," I say. "I fought them all alone while you smoked your hookah?"

"It's a good one, trust me." He takes a drag. "Moroccan tobacco, brewed and chewed and extracted from a forty-year-old virgin plant."

I turn and look at Tom Truckle hiding behind the trees. "It's time for you to talk to me." I pull him out.

"Not before you get me out of here," Tom says. "More of them are coming."

He is right about that. "All right, follow me."

I pull Tom with me toward the door, intending to keep using my skills to leave Oxford Asylum. The Pillar, however, keeps smoking in the garden.

"You're not coming?" I grimace.

"After you kill 'em all." He breathes out a curl of smoke in the air. "You're the one who has a triple black belt in None Fu. Welcome to the future, Alice."

# Chapter 30

As I continue using my unmatchable None Fu skills, Tom Truckle hides behind me. He also answers some of my questions. It's a weird way to have a conversation, but I want to know all about him.

"It's my fault we lost the Wonderland War," he says, as I strangle a few Reds.

"We?" I punch another. "Since when were you on the Inklings side?"

"There is so much you don't know about me."

"Better talk now, or I'll do to you what I am doing to them." I smash Reds into each other. "How come you're the Mock Turtle? You're a Wonderlander?"

"A neglected one, actually." He ducks behind me. "No one ever noticed me back then."

"I guess that's why Lewis wrote so briefly about you."

"Even though I inspired the famous mock turtle soup."

"Don't flatter yourself." I somersault and kick two Reds in midair. "Its taste sucks. Who eats turtle soup?"

"That's why I decided I'd be the director of an insane asylum," he says. "Among the Mushroomers who fear and respect me."

"I doubt that. They thought you were the maddest one in the asylum."

"I don't care what they thought. I had a plan."

"A plan?"

"Of course. I was supposed to connect with all asylums in the world and make sure they were filled with sane people."

"What kind of plan was that? Who told you that?"

"Lewis told me to."

# Chapter 31

I turn back and glare at him, choking a Red with one hand. With all of my skills, I wonder how we lost the war. "Don't lie to me, Turtle!"

"I'm not," he says. "Look behind you."

I do, pulling Tom up with me while I'm doing another parkour move in the asylum's corridor.

"Lewis wanted to guarantee the Inklings win the war. He set alternative plans everywhere to help the cause," he says. "One day, when I was crying myself to death in Wonderland, he offered me a chance to be a hero."

"You?" I don't know if I am supposed to believe him. Shouldn't it be me who becomes the hero?

"It was a long shot. The plan was that I collect the sanest scientists, teachers, and useful men and women into an asylum."

"Are you saying the Mushroomers were sane?"

"In the beginning, yes. Although spending too much time in the asylum messed with their minds."

"That's the most stupid plan I ever heard."

"It's not. Lewis knew the Queen would wreak havoc on the sane world, spreading the insane everywhere. Remember how mad the world already was when you were in the asylum? The wars, the poverty, and sickness? The Queen of Hearts has been planning this since long ago, even before she posed as the Queen of England."

"Go on." I punch another Red, advancing in the corridor. "Be brief."

"I framed sane people into being insane, so I could get them into the asylum," he says. "Of course, they weren't supposed to know that. Who'd have believed me when I told them about Wonderland?"

"Are you saying I was framed into thinking I'm mad?"

Tom shrugs, pulls out a pill, and swallows it in the middle of my fighting. "I'll explain all about you, but last."

"Why? I want to know what you know about me now."

"You have to hear the rest first."

I am too busy to argue, having reached the vast Tom Quad. The garden is thronged with too many Reds waiting for me. I have incredible None Flu skills, but even Bruce Lee can't fight an army.

"I kept framing sane people. I even created the Hole, where the March Hare was kept," Tom continues. "Lewis had told me he was so valuable he needed to be kept away from the Queen and Black Chess."

"Can't you just summarize the story?" I am busy now, fighting aimlessly, with hopes of reaching the door at the Tom Tower. Once we reach it, we'll be out of here. "I get it. Lewis ordered you to collect the sane people and keep them in the asylum, so when the Wonderland Wars came we'd have a secret army, disguised as mad people. I changed my mind now; the plan seems brilliant because it'd go undetected by Black Chess. But you said you were the reason why we lost the war. Why, Tom?"

"The pills," he says. "Life in the asylum was driving me mad. My kids and wife hated me, and Lewis denied me the luxury to tell anyone about it."

# Chapter 32

"Not even me?" I say. "If you were on my side, you should have told me. Why did you resist the Pillar when he asked for me to kill Wonderland Monsters?"

"Like I said, I'll be getting into that part later. What matters now is that when I took those pills, I didn't know they had side effects."

"Don't tell me you forgot things."

"I did."

In the middle of my war, I try not to panic. It has been one of my worries that the Lullaby pills messed with my head. Now, Tom is proof I was right.

"Slowly I forgot who I am," he explains. "Not like a clean slate, but visions came and went from me. One minute I remembered my purpose in life, another I didn't. But in the later days when you and the Pillar were always leaving the asylum, I began to realize I had a purpose. That I had been told to do this, though I was not quite sure who told me. Then when Carolus Ludovicus came to London, I remembered that I was supposed to protect the Mushroomers. I remembered everything and was about to lock the asylum and protect them all until the Cheshire snuck in and suspected I was a Wonderlander. I guess he knew when he tried to possess my soul and couldn't."

"So why did you cause us to lose the war?" I'm nearer to the gate now.

"Because I sold myself to Black Chess at the last moment."

"What? After all that Lewis told you?"

"It's a complicated story. I was forced to do it. As a result, the Mushroomers were killed and the Inklings had no real army to face Black Chess. I'm really sorry."

"Damn it, Turtle." I pull him harder and kick the last two Reds away, then we rush outside the gate. "I need to hear more, but we need an escape vehicle first."

"Which one?" There are a lot of damaged cars lined up outside.

"Like this one." I smile, pointing at the Pillar's fire truck.

I run toward it, Tom behind me, but I still have a question I can't keep for later. "So if the pills made you forget, how about the pills you fed me in the asylum?"

Tom shrugs again. I wonder what he is keeping from me. I reach for the truck's door handle, climb up, and pull Tom with me. As I am about to get into the driver's seat, I find the Pillar waiting inside, tapping the wheel and staring at his watch. "Seven minutes and thirty-nine seconds." He pouts, staring at his watch. "With a triple belt in None Fu, you should do better than that."

"Don't make me punch you in the face." I climb down and pace around to the other door. I push Tom up, squeeze him between me and the Pillar, then lock the door behind me.

"You haven't answered my question, Tom." I grab him by his sleeve as the Pillar guns down the road. "What about my pills?"

"They were Lullaby pills." Tom chokes, glancing at the Pillar. I wonder why.

"Like Carolus?" I ask.

Tom nods, but the Pillar ignores his gaze.

"Are you saying I have an evil Alice doppelgänger?"

"I don't..." He hesitates. "It's complicated."

"Talk or I swear I will kill you, Tom."

One last gaze at the Pillar then he spits it out: "The Lullaby pills were meant for you to..."

And there, when I am about to hear a crucial truth about my past, I suddenly bleed from the nose, feeling disoriented and dizzy. My hands loosen up and my head falls on one shoulder.

"Alice?" The Pillar sounds worried. "What's going on?"

"I — " My eyes meet his. I'm most perplexed and confused. Did one of the Reds stab me? "I think I'm going to faint."

The Pillar orders Tom to take the wheel. He scoots over and examines me. "No, Alice, it's not that."

"What is it, then?"

"You're dying, Alice," the Pillar says.

"What do you mean I'm dying? You said I'm not hit."

"It's not the Reds who attempted to kill you." The Pillar's jaw tenses. "It's those who sent you to the future."

"Mr. Tick and Mrs. Tock?" My eyes widen.

"I think they fooled us both," the Pillar says. "They sent you here to die."

# Chapter 33

"What a frabjous trick, Mrs. Tock," Mr. Tick said, sipping his six o'clock tea — although it wasn't six o'clock yet.

"I'm flattered you liked it, Mr. Tick," said Mrs. Tock. "For a man who always ticks on time, a woman who tocks too late is most delighted."

"She is suffering now, right?" He pointed at the spasming Alice on the bed in the back room of the Inklings.

"Beautifully." Mrs. Tock snickered. "Soon she'll spit blood."

"It's a remarkable achievement, I have to say," Mr. Tick said. "Not since the invention of time have I been so impressed. Imagine her dying in both the future and the past at once."

"Mind-boggling, right?" She whizzed a hand next to her head.

"I have to be honest with you," Mr. Tick said. "Although I always arrive sharply on time, I never really understood *time*."

"How so, Mr. Tick?"

"For example, what time is it right now?"

"It's twelve thirty in the afternoon."

"Is that the time now? Are you sure?"

"Positive."

"You just think so. That was the time when you checked your watch a few seconds ago," Mr. Tick pointed out. "But between learning what the time is and telling it to me, you were already three or four seconds late. So you basically didn't tell me the real time. Meaning no one can really arrive *on time*."

"Aha." Mrs. Tock had always been confused by the idea. No wonder she preferred to arrive later.

"Also, it's around twelve thirty here in Oxford, but not so in Cambridge," Mr. Tick said. "I very much believe time is an impostor."

"I agree, Mr. Tick. Look at poor Alice here. She is dying in the now and in the *later*," she said. "But wait a minute, aren't we time?"

"No, Mrs. Tock." He sipped his tea. "I'm Mr. Tick. You're Mrs. Tock. We work for time. Remember?"

"I always forget. Forgive me. I prefer we skip this conversation," Mrs. Tock said. "I think men like Einstein are an expert on time."

"Really? Did you ever see his hair? Time drove him mad. He only fooled us into thinking he knew about it," Mr. Tick said. "So tell me, what's the plan from here on?" He pointed at Alice.

"She is dying because there is a limit for the time an individual stay in the future," Mrs. Tock explained.

"Does she know that?"

"Of course not. We didn't tell her. What'd be the fun in that?"

"And if she wants to come back, what does she have to do?"

"Two things. First, someone has to inject her with a Lullaby serum so she can make it back to our present time."

"Which I suppose the Pillar has the resources to accomplish in the future, right?"

"Indeed. Or we wouldn't have let him think that he managed to visit the future through the Tom Tower," Mrs. Tock said. "The poor bastard doesn't know that I secretly helped him do it."

"And he has no idea Margaret intentionally made him listen to her conversation, either." Mr. Tick sipped his tea. "Ingenious plan, Mrs. Tock."

"Thank you, Mr. Tick." Mrs. Tock blushed. Mr. Tick hadn't flattered her since about two hundred years ago.

"But from what I know, it's impossible to evade death after time-traveling," Mr. Tick said. "I mean, even if she returns, she will die within a few hours in our time."

"That's true, Mr. Tick. That's why there is only one way to save her life if she manages to make it to the past."

"What is it, Mrs. Tock?" He put the tea aside. "I'm most punctually, accurately, and timingly curious."

"Alice can only live if she finds her Wonder."

Mr. Tick's eyes shone brightly. The three hairies on his head bent like a banana peel. "You don't say."

"It's true. The only way she can see another day is if she finds her Wonder."

"Which we both know is almost impossible."

"Yes, I know." Mrs. Tock snickered, shrugging her broad shoulders. "But let's not get ahead of ourselves. Let's first watch her come back from the future."

"If she ever manages to pull it off." Mr. Tick scanned Alice's spasming body, now slightly bleeding from her nose.

"Before we continue watching, Mr. Tick," Mrs. Tock said, "what about her?" She pointed at Fabiola standing frozen like a statue beside them. Mr. Tick had stopped time in the Inklings a few minutes ago, so Fabiola wouldn't bust them when she saw Alice dying. It actually added a lovely sense of quietness to the place. Mr. Tick and Mrs. Tock loved it when humans were quiet.

"I will unfreeze her later, Mrs. Tock." Mr. Tick began sipping his tea again. "After I drink my six o'clock tea. Oh, I feel like we have all the time in the world."

# Chapter 34

"Did you just say Mr. Tick and Mrs. Tock?" Tom drives the truck now. "Are you saying you're not the current Alice and the Pillar?"

"It depends on how you look at it," the Pillar says. "But if you're asking if we were sent from the past, then the answer is yes."

"Oh, my." Tom panics, turning the wheel. "This isn't right."

I can understand that as a Wonderlander Tom knows about the Tick and Tock couple. But why is he panicking? "What's wrong, Turtle?"

"Nothing." He shakes his head. "Not now. Let's see if there is a way to save your life first."

"I want to know what's going on!" I demand, but then my head aches again.

"Calm down." The Pillar wipes a trail of blood from my nose. "Or this is going to get worse."

I stare at the blood, my heart weakening. I think I can't hear it beat properly.

"There is only one way out of this," the Pillar says. "A Lullaby pill." He shifts his stare toward Tom.

"Why are you looking at me?"

"You're the director of the Radcliffe Asylum," I say, catching on. "You must know how to get a Lullaby pill."

"*Was* the director, about fourteen years ago," Tom says. "I've been trapped in the Oxford Asylum for the last five years for trying to lead the revolution."

As he mentions it, I glimpse the graffiti on the walls. *All hail the Mock Turtle. All hail the revolution.*

"This really bothers me," I mumble. "How is it that Tom Truckle leads the revolution in the future?" Now I am talking to the Pillar. "Why not me?"

"Calm down, Alice," the Pillar says. "Or I can't think of a way to get you the pill."

"Why not me?" I insist. "Aren't I the Real Alice?"

"I can explain…" Tom begins.

"Shut up!" the Pillar says. "First we have to save your life, then we look for answers, Alice. Look in my eyes and tell me you understand what I just said."

The Pillar is assertive, wanting to help me. I find myself nodding. Even the nodding hurts when I do it. What's going to happen to me?

"That's a start." The Pillar sighs and stares back at Tom. "Do you happen to know how long she has before she dies?"

"Once the bleeding begins, it takes a time traveler the same time he needs to eat a thousand marshmallows to die completely," Tom says.

"What does that even mean?" I retort.

"It's what the *Hitchhiker's Guide to Wonderlastic Time Travels* says," Tom explains. "I myself can eat ten marshmallows in a minute. Given that, I suppose it takes about — "

"Zip it, Turtle," the Pillar interjects. "Here is what's going to happen. See that motorcycle at the curb?"

"Yes?"

"Pull over there. I'll take it and find the pill."

"You're not going to leave me here, Pillar?" I ask him, as Tom pulls over.

"I'll be back," he says.

"Schwarzenegger used to say that. Now he is dead," Tom comments.

Neither of us even pay attention to him. The Pillar lowers his head and whispers in my ear, "Stay alive. You can do it."

He descends the truck and starts the motorcycle, disappearing into the streets.

Gathering what's left of my energy, I turn back to Tom. "I think now it's time to tell me more."

# Chapter 35

"It was the flamingo that converted me into working for Black Chess," Tom begins, still driving through the streets. He has to keep driving in case the Reds are still on our tail.

"The flamingo?"

"The one the Queen of Hearts sent to the asylum," he says. I didn't even know about it. "One day, I received an order from Her Majesty to cure a flamingo of hers."

"Cure it? In an asylum?"

"The poor animal didn't succumb to her orders, and wouldn't let her use it as a mallet in a croquet game. She thought the flamingo had psychological issues and wanted it healed into submission."

"Healed into submission? What kind of healing is that?"

"The Wonderland style. Anyways, I found nothing wrong with it, and began to befriend it," Tom says. "In my darkest hour when I had no one to talk to, it became my best friend."

"What does all this nonsense have to do with losing the war?"

"The flamingo was the Queen's bait." Tom averts his eyes from mine, and keeps them on the road. It's easy to see he truly regrets his past and wishes to become someone better. Every passing moment, I am more able to believe he did actually lead the revolution.

"Bait?"

"The preposterous Queen fooled me," he says. "She knew who I was. She knew of Lewis' mission. And she was the one who put the pills into my coffee and mock turtle soups until I became an addict."

I am speechless. The Queen of Hearts has always struck me as stupid, impulsive, and borderline naive, like an angry child farting its way through life. I never thought of her as a planner with hidden agendas. I thought she was just mad at the world because of the circus. "I still don't understand the flamingo's role in having you work for Black Chess."

"I guess your IQ just dropped because you're dying, Alice," he says. "The flamingo became my best friend, the one I trusted, talked to all the time. I told it about the things I remembered, the exact details of Lewis' plan. More shattering than anything else is that at some point the flamingo talked telepathically to me, poisoning my thoughts until I weakened and joined Black Chess in exchange for a reputable position in Parliament. A position where I could be respected, feared, pay my children's tuition, and get back my wife."

"And the flamingo, what happened to it?"

"Don't you know?" He glances at me. "The Queen chopped off its head after that. There are signposts everywhere about the incident."

"I saw it."

Suddenly, Tom's glance turns into a glare, as if seeing a ghost.

"What is it?"

"The Reds." He speeds up. "They're after us again."

# Chapter 36

## *THE FUTURE: MOUNT CEMETERY, GUILDFORD*

The Pillar felt the rush of wind slapping him in the face while he drove. The cemetery was only a mile or two away now. He was risking Alice's life by driving this fast to come here. After all, Mount Cemetery was about two hours away from where he had left Alice. But he had bet on the illogical Wonderlastic rules of time traveling. According to the *Hitchhiker's Guide to Wonderlastic Time Travels*, distance sometimes meant nothing when time travelers were in different times than where they actually lived. It was the same reason why Alice managed to get from London to Oxford by walking a few streets. According to the book, a traveler could get anywhere he or she wished with good intentions and determination.

Whatever that meant, the Pillar thought. He didn't care how nonsense worked. What mattered was that it worked. It only took him twenty minutes to arrive.

He didn't want to give in to thinking about time, and its complications, for too long. After all, time was a loop. A wheel rebirthing and reinventing itself all the time. Which meant he and Alice must have been here before.

But he was thankful he couldn't remember it, or he would have gone really mad. He thought how perception of time, and life, was nothing but a point of view. It wasn't real, but there was nothing anyone could do about it. All one could do was live the moment they believed — probably deceivingly — was the present.

He parked the motorcycle and took off his goggles.

Then he jogged toward the gates of Mount Cemetery, not surprised at its decaying form. It was almost buried in vines and crawling insects. No one paid attention or respect to Lewis Carroll's burial place in the future — and not much in the present, either.

Why would they, when Black Chess's winning of the war was all about bringing the man's legacy down?

The Pillar stepped through the shrubs and the mud until he found a crack in the walls. The sky greyed and boomed with rain as he entered the cemetery.

Inside, it wasn't easy locating Carroll's burial plot. The cemetery looked like it had been a battlefield at some point in the Wonderland Wars.

The Pillar took off his blue coat, folded it carefully, and placed it at the cleanest place he came across. He pulled back his sleeves, showing his aging skin, peeling off day by day. Something he didn't want anyone else to see. He didn't see the point of anyone knowing about his sickness.

After all, why would anyone care?

He located a shovel and walked to the spot where he believed Lewis was buried.

"Sorry for digging you up, mate," he whispered to the grave. "I need the one thing you took with you to the grave. The Lullaby pills."

# Chapter 37

## THE FUTURE: OXFORD STREETS

Tom is a terrible driver. If he keeps driving this way, we're either going to crash into something or get caught by the Reds who are chasing us on motorcycles now.

"Give me the wheel." I push him over.

"But you're bleeding."

"I can't None Fu while I'm dying, but I think I can still drive. Look for a gun or something in the back. Do something useful."

"There is a sleeping dog in the back," Tom says.

I smile when he says that. That dog was so hungry that when he was fed he felt good enough to sleep through such a chase. "Don't wake him up," I say. "Just find a gun and start shooting at the Reds."

"There is nothing back there, only water hoses."

I use a lot of what's left of my power to stare back at him, hoping he will get the message.

Tom smirks and tilts his head. He knuckles his fingers and pops a few pills. "You're thinking what I'm thinking?"

"Glad to know you're smart enough to think what *I am thinking*." I veer the truck against a couple of motorcycles and squeeze them against a wall.

"Water hose wars it is," Tom chirps like a child. What can I say? He's a Wonderlander, after all.

Behind me, he starts hitting the Reds with full-throttle water bullets.

"You remember I'm here for the keys, don't you?" I shout back.

"I know." He struggles with the pumping hose, but is doing a good job at keeping the Reds at bay. "That's what I was going to ask about. How did you find me?"

"I found the note."

"What note?"

"The one where I kept your address with a scribbling saying that I kept the keys with you."

"I don't know what you're talking about, Alice."

"What do you mean? We must have had a deal or something. I must have kept the keys with you after the war. Or why do I have this note?"

"True, I was in possession of the keys once." He sounds like he is keeping something from me again. "But you couldn't have possibly made a note to come and take them from me."

"Why not?" I want to face him but I am busy with the wheel, totally ignoring my bleeding nose, although my blood is staining the wheel by now, and my vision is dimming.

"Because you know I lost the Six Keys a long time ago."

"What?" I almost hit the brakes. "You lost the keys?"

"Not that they are of any particular use anymore. We lost the war when the Queen grabbed hold of the Six Keys," Tom says. "But you already know I lost the keys. Oh, wait. I mean the real version of you in this world knows that. Of course, you don't know, because you're not really from this time."

I am too dizzy to think about this paradoxical situation. "I just want to know how you lost the keys, and how come I found this note."

Tom takes a moment to think it over. I trust he has figured out the puzzle. "I get it now."

"What is it? Please tell me, because nothing makes sense in this future anymore."

"Mr. Tick and Mrs. Tock."

"What about them?"

"They don't really want you to die," Tom speculates. "They wanted everything that happened to happen the way it did."

"How so?"

"They have access to the future. They planted the note so you'd follow it, because they knew I stole the keys from you."

"You stole them." The truck bumps against something on the road. I speed up to cross it, realizing I have so little strength in me now. "I thought I gave them to you."

"Don't worry about this part," Tom says. "What matters is that Mr. Tick and Mrs. Tock, or whoever hired them, thought I have the keys, and wanted to find them through you. They planted the note because they knew I wouldn't open up to anyone, even you, about their location."

"Even me?" I am dizzy, not sure if I am catching every word, barely able to drive ahead. "Why wouldn't you tell me about their location?"

"Because in this future I trust no one. You could be the Cheshire disguised, for all I know — and don't talk to me about him being unable to possess Wonderlanders," Tom says. "I am only opening up to you because I know you're from the past, because if you find the keys and put them in the right hands, you can change the future."

"And that's what they want exactly," I say. "They want me to return with the keys so they can take them from me."

"You're getting the picture now. Think of it—why isn't there another Alice from the future? They must have done something to her so she wouldn't warn you or tell you the truth."

"It's hard to really comprehend all of this," I say. "But I get their plan to get the keys now. I get it that they thought you'd give me the keys only when you realized I am from the past. What puzzles me is how you lost the keys."

"Didn't exactly lose them," he says. "I handed them to the wrong person."

"Who?" I enter a dark tunnel, wishing I could lose the Reds in here.

"I gave them to Jack."

And with that the darkness drapes its curtain of deception down on me. Because let's face it. In the future, Jack is not Jack. He is the Cheshire, fooling Tom. Having fooled me as well, making me think that Jack affected him so much he loved me. The Cheshire never changed. A nobody, disguising in people he meets, parasitizing on their thoughts and emotions, just like the sneakiest of devils.

My hands give up on the wheel. My strength withers. And I fall down on my head.

# Chapter 38

## *The Future: Mount Cemetery, Guildford*

The Pillar was digging with all his might. As fast as he could. Sweating and panting. He'd never felt the need to save someone like he needed to save Alice now.

And there it was, finally, Carroll's corpse, lying on its back, strangely mummified, looking as if he were still alive. The Pillar wasn't surprised. Carroll was full of surprises. He wouldn't discard the possibility that the famous mathematician had found an embalming method like the ancient Egyptians.

The Pillar knelt down to reach for Carroll's pockets. The dead man's shoulders snapped, just a little, probably an odd reflex of muscles being exposed to oxygen or light.

"Relax," the Pillar told him. "I'm just here for the Pills. She needs them or she will die."

But Carroll's dead body snapped again, as if not wanting him to reach for them.

"Look," the Pillar said. "I know you don't want her to take the pills, not in the future, but I can help her."

The corpse still stiffened, its arm bent awkwardly. The Pillar needed to break it to get to the pills.

"Aren't you the one who kept showing up in her dreams? Didn't you meet her in the Tom Tower? Didn't you meet her back in Wonderland through the Einstein Blackboard? And after the circus, she said she saw you with the Inklings." The Pillar talked to Carroll's corpse as if it were alive. "Didn't you show up to her in the Inkling, thanking her for saving you from Carolus and telling her she is the Real Alice?"

The corpse didn't move—and, of course, it didn't talk back.

The Pillar wasn't sure what was going on. He didn't want to break Carroll's arm to get the pill. But, looking at his watch, he knew he was losing time.

"She will die, Carroll," Pillar said in Carroll's ear. "This future is a mistake. What's done is done. I can go back and save her.

She doesn't have to take the same route again. She just messed up."

The corpse's hand stiffened even more.

"It's not her fault, Carroll," the Pillar pleaded. "Let me help her. She saved your life, for God's sake. This is only a possible future. You of all people know this. We can always change the future." The Pillar was fighting a tear, threatening to break his lifetime record of never crying, not once.

He gently put his hands on Carroll's chest. "For the sake of the good memories, Carroll," the Pillar said. "Don't let what happened after the circus do this to you. She needs to live, find the keys, and save the world. For the sake of your memories with her in the garden in Christ Church."

Carroll's stiffened hands loosened a bit at the Pillar's last words.

"Remember those days, her playing in garden, behind the door to Wonderland? Remember her fluttering hair, the sparkling eyes of a child who loved rabbits and turtles? The girl who hated books without pictures and lived in the minds of every child in the world until this day?"

Carroll's hands shifted, giving way for the Pillar to reach for the pills. They were still intact inside a plastic bag in his chest pocket. Three pills. Probably preserved in the same manner Carroll's corpse was.

The Pillar took the pills and tucked them in his back pocket. He grabbed for the shovel and said, "Now it's time to bury you again, old man." He sighed. "Not that burying your corpse lessens your presence in the world. Somehow you're immortal."

A few minutes later, the job was done. The Pillar rolled his sleeves back down and put on his suit. He walked out toward the motorcycle, counting on the trick of time to get back to Alice as soon as he could.

On his way, he stumbled across a set of tombstones outside the church. He was sure they hadn't been here in the past, and wondered who was buried next to Carroll. Who died in the future and deserved this burial place?

The Pillar stepped up and read the name on the tombstone. It didn't make sense, but it hurt reading that name. Someone was going to die in the future, sooner than anyone would have expected.

And boy, what a loss that would be.

# Chapter 39

## *THE FUTURE: OXFORD STREETS*

Every now and then I manage to open my eyes for a few seconds. Dying is a horrible thing. I feel I am being stripped of everything I have, one second after the other. My skin, my vision, my hearing, my breath, and my soul. All is withering away.

The fire truck seems to have been flipped on its side, because I see things at a ninety-degree angle. Tom is in an awkward position, firing the water hose in all directions. But it doesn't look like a lasting plan.

I see the poor dog, now awake, swimming in a pool of puddles, trying to escape the Reds' bullets. Bandersnatch bullets. If I could just stand up to save the poor thing from the human madness...

But I can't. My eyelids droop on me again. It's so hard to flip them open again. It's like pushing open a gate of steel.

"No!" I hear Tom scream.

My vision is almost gone.

The only thought that comes to me is: What kind of a lame hero am I?

No wonder I'm not leading the revolution in the future. I am assuming I wasn't up to the mission and failed somehow. That's why I am hiding beyond the walls of a so-called Wonderland compound. What kind of future scenario is that?

And my children? How can I leave them like this? I am really hoping Tom is right, that there is another version of me, a real responsible mother, who will take care of Tiger and Lily in this life.

As for me, it looks like my time has come. It wasn't such a bad ride, I tell myself. I saved a few lives, didn't I? Of course, I killed those on the bus earlier, but like the tattoo on my arm rants: I can't go back to yesterday because... blah blah blah.

A shot resonates in my head. A scream follows. Adrenalin pumps into my thin veins, a little push that helps me open my eyes again.

"I'm here, Alice," a voice tells me. It's the Pillar. "I've got the pills."

"Really?" I cough blood.

"I just need to straighten you up and shelter you somewhere safe, or a stray bullet could end us both." He begins to pull me into a shaded area. I can't make out what is what. The world is upside down, skewed and ridiculous.

"That's it." He lays me back against the truck's front, I believe. "Can you swallow it?" He tucks the pill into my mouth.

I shake my head, realizing my jaw has tightened. I can hardly give the pill a kick with my tongue.

"Don't worry," the Pillar says, pulling something nearby. "Thankfully, we're in a fire truck."

I don't understand what this means. The pill is melting on my tongue, but I can't swallow it. What's worse than that?

"Here." He pulls the water hose and drowns my face with water. "That's why I'm thankful."

The water splashes on my face and the pill slides inside me. I will be forever grateful to the Pillar. Maybe I can return to the past and fix this messed-up future.

But I am not feeling better.

"Alice?" The Pillar begins to shake me violently.

I can't even feel his hands now. I am withering away. The pills aren't the answer to saving my life.

# Chapter 40

"So the pills won't work?" Mr. Tick put his teacup aside and wiped his thin lips with a napkin.

"I made sure they're taken," Mrs. Tock explained.

"Taken?"

"I've had someone pull them out of Carroll's pockets," she said. "The ones the Pillar will find, if he so takes that route to save her, are water pills. Useless, just like diet pills."

"Pretty cruel." Mr. Tick tucked a napkin into the collar of his vest, getting ready for his six o'clock brownie. "And fabulous, I must admit. I can't tell you how much you have entertained me today."

"My pleasure, Mr. Tick."

"So the girl dies now?"

"You know we don't want that to happen." Mrs. Tock snickered, reaching for a piece of Mr. Tick's brownie. He slapped her hand away. "Alice needs to live. We're just preparing her for the big showdown, so we can get the keys."

"Poor girl." He gorged on his brownie. "She has no idea what's going on."

"It's the only way to get the keys."

"And to know if she's really the Real Alice," Mr. Tick remarked.

"That too, of course," she said. "According to the *Hitchhiker's Guide to Wonderlastic Time Travels*, she will die in the future if she is not the Real Alice."

"And if she survives?"

"There is a possibility she might be Alice."

"That's rather contradictory. If she dies, she isn't Alice, but if she lives, she *may* be Alice?"

"Wonderland logic. Can't argue with that," she said. "It's as confusing as the concept of time."

"Whatever." He waved a hand after downing the last piece of the brownie. "I'm curious to see how it plays out."

"Me too, Mr. Tick."

"But I'm starting to get bored again," Mr. Tick said. "Not that I haven't been entertained by this piece of time travel. But I feel there isn't much pain involved. I need to see tragedies. People in dire pain and agony."

"I understand. Seeing people in agony makes you tick, Mr. Tick." She chuckled. "I have an idea. Why not stop time from freezing inside the Inklings?"

"Why would I do that?"

"You'd wake up Fabiola." Mrs. Tock snickered and shrugged. "This way, you can see her suffer when she sees Alice spasming and coughing blood."

"What a brilliant idea, Mrs. Tock," Mr. Tick said, and snapped his fingers to unfreeze the White Queen.

# Chapter 41

## THE FUTURE: OXFORD STREETS

"Alice!" I still hear the Pillar screaming.

I'm sinking into my own rabbit hole toward the other side of the spectrum of life.

"Is she going to die?" I think that's Tom shouting, but I'm not sure.

Then someone arrives — I think.

"What are you doing here?" the Pillar roars at the guest.

"I can save her." I think I know the voice, but can't focus hard enough to remember.

"Another trick of yours," Tom says. "Go away."

"I always have a few tricks in my sleeves," that someone says. "I'd even admit I switched the pills on Carroll's corpse."

"What corpse?" Tom asks.

What are they talking about? Who is this stranger?

"That's why she is dying." The Pillar sounds angry. "I'm going to kill you."

"No need to," the stranger says. "I have her cure. The real pills."

Really? Am I going to live?

"And what do you ask in return?" the Pillar says.

"I've always liked your practical methods, Pillar," the stranger says. "I'm going to give her the pills if she promises me a favor."

"Whatever it takes, Cheshire," the Pillar says. "Just give them to me."

"Don't call me Cheshire, please," the Cheshire says in Jack's voice. "I'm neither the Cheshire nor Jack now. I'm both. Not as naive and hapless in love as Jack, nor am I hating humans like the Cheshire."

"And I've seen this sentimental rubbish of a movie before. Spare me the bullshit and hand me the goddamn pills," the Pillar says.

"She has to listen to what I want first," the Cheshire, or Jack, demands. "I know you think I'm still working for Black Chess because I fooled Tom and took the keys from him, but you're wrong."

"Then what's right? Enlighten me." The Pillar is impatient.

"I stole the keys so I can have my bargain with Alice."

"Bargain?"

"Yes, bargain. The keys and her life in exchange for Jack's life."

"Jack is dead," Tom interjects. "Even long before you possessed his body."

"That's what Alice has to fix for me if I give her the pills," the Cheshire says. "She has to time-travel to the past and let Jack live."

I reach out a feeble hand, not seeing where it's pointing.

"What's wrong, Alice?" the Pillar asks.

I try my best to keep my hand steady, until the Cheshire gets the message and reaches back for me. Not the Cheshire, really. But Jack. I squeeze his hand. I understand what's going on. This Cheshire/Jack mix produced a different person who cherishes his life and blames me for killing him. Even fourteen years later, this new person demands to live. If time travel works for finding keys, then it should work for saving life.

All Jack is asking me is not to kill him on the bus. He wants me to go back in time and stop the accident. I want it, too. I've always felt guilty for killing Jack. It's time to correct the past.

Jack's hand warms up. I think he feels me somehow. Slowly, I feel another pill tucked in my mouth. It's the right pill; I know it. It tastes like those I took back in the asylum.

"Promise me you'll save my life, Alice," Jack demands.

"I promise, Jack," I say. "I'm really sorry I killed you."

# Chapter 42

Life seeps back through the pores of my skin, the veins in my head, and the blood in my heart. Funny how we're not grateful for breathing until the time comes when it's our last breath.

The Pillar helps me straighten up again, brushing my hair back. "Are you all right?"

"All right? I'm not sure." I chuckle. "But I'll live."

The dog comes and licks my face, welcoming me back to life — or should I say the future?

Tom just stands there, saying nothing. He has that look which I can't understand. He exchanges brief mutters with the Pillar then turns back to me. It's almost as if he's not so happy I am alive.

But I don't have the capacity to interpret what's behind all of this.

Jack stands with a straight face piercing through me. This isn't Jack. This isn't the Cheshire. It's someone in between. Who'd have thought? The most lovable boy possessed by the most vicious cat.

"Thank you," I tell him.

"Don't thank me," he says. "Just save me. Do all you can to make Mr. Tick and Mrs. Tock help you go back in time and save me — save the bus, Alice."

"I don't even remember why I did it." I want the Jack inside the Cheshire to warm up to me, but he doesn't.

"No excuses," he says. "I don't care if you don't remember. I care if you save me instead of me ending up sacrificing myself for you and later getting possessed by this vicious cat in me."

I realize that if I can go back in time and save the bus, Jack will never get possessed by the Cheshire for fourteen years. It makes me want to do it more. But I still have a question. "Since fourteen years have passed, Jack, I only want to know why you came back for me. You said you wanted to tell me something, warn me about something—or someone. I believe I have the right to know before I go back in time."

Jack doesn't answer me. He exchanges another look with Tom and the Pillar and then turns and walks away.

I reach for him, but I'm still a bit tired. I don't even have time to cry. The Reds arrive and surround me, Tom, and the Pillar.

A pressure-filled moment passes, all of us staring at each other. I'm surprised the Reds don't attack us.

"You're really hard to catch, Mrs. Wonder," a Red leader says to me. "We weren't going to kill you under any circumstances. We just know you don't belong here."

"What do you mean?"

"No more games, please," the Red says. "We know you're from the past. You and Mr. Pillar."

"How do you — "

"It doesn't matter how we know," the Red says. "We just want you to leave our world and go back where you came from. That's Mr. Jay's orders."

"Mr. Jay?"

"You don't have to know about him. Not at the moment. Somewhere in the past you'll meet him, and you'll understand a lot of things. Now, would you mind?"

"I will leave." I nod, eyeing the Pillar. He nods at the dog. "What about him?" I say.

"After you've taken the pill, all you have to do to leave is kiss the dog on the mouth, and he'll be all right," the Pillar explains, shaking his shoulders.

"That's silly," I say.

"Blame it on the Hitchhiker's Guide to Wonderlastic Time Travels."

# Chapter 43

Fabiola stood outside her bar, smoking a cigarette. She tapped her foot impatiently, waiting for the Pillar.

The eccentric professor arrived with his cane and a pout on his face. "Is she alive?"

"She is." Fabiola killed the cigarette on the ground. "Those two lunatics, Mr. Tick and Mrs. Tock, were just messing with her mind. Yours, too."

"Why would they do that?" the Pillar asked. "Entertaining themselves?"

"Worse. It's a trick. A master plan by whoever hired them."

"I'm not doubting that at all. They fooled me into listening to Margaret's conversation, and made me think I managed to time-travel through the Tom Tower when it was the doing of the Tick and Tock couple. The question is why."

"Because according to some book concerning the rules of Wonderland time travel, whoever cheats death in the future is vulnerable to die within the next twenty-four hours as a consequence."

"So getting the keys from the future was only a game?"

"I can't believe we fell for their trick," Fabiola said. "The keys can only be found in the past where Alice hid him them. Now Alice is obliged to travel to the past to get the keys and save her life. That's what it's all about."

"How can she save her life in the past?"

"By finding something called the Wonder."

The Pillar shrugged. Fabiola realized he knew what it was. "What's the Wonder?"

"Something she shouldn't find," he said stiffly.

"What does that mean?" She was about to lash out at him again. Deep inside, she didn't want to have this conversation with him. But she had to, so she could save Alice's life, if possible.

"It's a paradox. Two things that contradict each other. She won't live if she doesn't find her Wonder, and horrible things will happen to her if she does."

"Don't do this to me, Pillar. Don't play those games with me."

"Let's not fight, Fabiola. Not now."

"Then what do you suggest we do?"

"We have no choice," the Pillar said. "Alice has to go back to fit into whatever plan they cooked up for her. She needs to get the keys and find her Wonder. The rest of the consequences are going to shatter us all. But they're undeniable now. I'm such a fool. I should've read between the lines."

"You messed up, Carter," Fabiola said. Only she called him by his first name. Only she knew him well enough to do that. "Why don't you just leave us be?"

"It's you who called for me, Fabiola. Remember?"

"I hate you so much," she said, gripping the door.

"Nothing new with that," the Pillar said. "You always did. In return, I've always loved you."

"Don't start!" She loosened her grip and waved her other hand at him. "Just don't. You don't even know why I hate you now? It doesn't have anything to do with the past. This is about now."

"Why do you hate me now, Fabiola?" The Pillar sighed.

"Because this girl inside apparently isn't Alice," Fabiola said. "I've forced myself to pretend she was, over and over again. I tried to make it easy on her and not tell her the truth. And now, the poor girl is risking her life, and for what? If she dies within twenty-four hours it's going to be your fault."

"I'm aware of that," the Pillar said without the slightest hint of sympathy. She couldn't stand him being so cruel — or was he just too tough? "This still doesn't justify why you hate me so much right now. What is it, really?"

Fabiola hesitated then said, "Because I love her. The girl is energy of light. Smart, ambitious, and has a heart of heroes."

She stamped one foot on the ground. "I bloody love her. And I swear to God, I'll kill you if anything happens to her."

Fabiola wiped away her tears and prepared to go back inside. She hated it when her anger surfaced like that. She had sworn not to give in to the woman she was in the past. Back in Wonderland, when she wasn't a nun or a bartender, but the bravest of warriors.

"Fabiola," the Pillar called after her. "When it's over, I'll be in Tom Quad in Oxford University."

"So what?"

"I think you'll want to see me once Alice returns to the past. Something horrible is going to happen then. We'll have to talk about it."

"You arrogant prick," she said. "Why are you always sure of yourself? I don't want to see you ever again."

"If I had a mushroom for every time I heard you say this." The Pillar rolled his cane in the air and walked away. "I'll be waiting in Tom Quad. Trust me, you'll come."

# Chapter 44

I'm back to the present life. My name is Alice and I hardly know who I really am. Names are the just the layer on top. You peel it off and there is the real you beneath. Have you ever seen the real you? Have you ever tried to?

Now that I'm back from the future, Fabiola returns to the Inklings, helping me drink a lot of water, cleaning off all the blood from my nose. She helps me sit and hands me a cup of milk and some food. We're alone in the back room, waiting for Mr. Tick and Mrs. Tock to return. Although I want to smash their heads against the wall, there is nothing I can do to them. They're practically immortal. I hate time so much right now.

"What about the March Hare?" I say.

"He's still unconscious, but not dead," Fabiola says. "The creepy couple forcefully leak some of their magic tea into his mouth every now and then, so he stays alive."

"But that's not the real antidote that will bring him back to life. Right?"

"It isn't." She wipes off my sweat. "And we don't know how to get it. Listen, Alice, you don't have to do this."

"Go back in time?" I say. "Of course I have to."

"Maybe the March Hare's time has come in this life. Maybe it's his time to die."

I can't believe she said that. I can't forget the image of the Columbian children gathered around his bed, crying their eyes out. But Fabiola isn't herself anymore. She is slowly morphing into whoever she was in Wonderland. I am beginning to think she was borderline heartless in Wonderland. A good warrior, but sometimes heartless.

"It's not just about the March Hare," I tell her.

"Don't tell me it's about the keys. We can find them one by one in this world."

"Not just the keys. I'm going to die if I don't find my Wonder, remember?"

"And we don't have an idea what it is." Fabiola scowls.

"That's why we need to talk to Mr. Tick and Mrs. Tock again. They want me to go back to get the keys. But I'm not doing it until they tell me what my Wonder is." I don't tell Fabiola that I promised Jack I'd save his life in the past. I don't think she'd like that. All in all, there seems to be all kinds of reasons for me to go back in time.

Mr. Tick and Mrs. Tock open the door and enter the room. They smile and sit on their chairs opposite each other, as if nothing bad ever happened. Time will always smile at you, even when it's ripping you of the days and nights of your life.

"She is a strong girl," Mr. Tick tells his wife, pointing at me. "I think she is up to the job."

"She may also be the Real Alice," Mrs. Tock says.

"I'm the Real Alice," I interrupt. "And stop talking to each other as if we're not in the room."

"Badass, too," Mr. Tick whispers to his wife. "I like her."

"But she isn't the Real Alice." Mrs. Tock rubs her chin. "We can't be really sure until she finds the keys in the past."

"Stop it." I am about to get up and scream at them. Fabiola holds me back. "Let's get into what matters," I say. "What the hell is my Wonder?"

"She's practical, too," Mr. Tick says to his wife.

"She probably got that from the Pillar," Mrs. Tock says. "But really, Mr. Tick, we should tell her about her Wonder."

"Agreed, Mrs. Tock." He turns back to me. "Your Wonder, Alice — everyone's Wonder, in fact — is the one thing you do in your life that you're most proud of. The one thing that when asked on your deathbed, 'What did you really bring to this life?' you'd tell us about."

# Chapter 45

"And how am I supposed to find that?"

"That's up to you," Mrs. Tock says. "While you're back in time, find the thing that if you do, it will be so important, and so good, that life will grant you an extension."

"Pretty shoddy, coming from two lunatics like you," Fabiola comments.

"Did she just call us shoddy, Mrs. Tock?" Mr. Tick says.

"I think she did. Although you always arrive on time, Mr. Tick."

"Remind me to kick their asses when I get back from the past, Ms. Fabiola," I say.

"Don't forget to call me, because I will kick them with you, Ms. Alice," Fabiola says, playing along.

"Badass. Practical. And sarcastic," Mr. Tick says. "I really want you to be the Real Alice."

"I am her." I am not sure if I am stubborn, fooling myself, but I have this feeling inside me. I'm the Real Alice. "So let's start. How do I go back in time?"

"First of all, take this." Mrs. Tock hands me a pink pill.

"What's that? Another Lullaby pill?"

"It's an address," Mr. Tick says. "The *Wonderlastic Guide of Time Travels* offers a solution for taking items back in time with you. And we need to give you an address. This pill will help you remember the address in the past."

I take it. "What address?"

"It's my address in the past," Mrs. Tock says. "You will need it in case something goes wrong."

"Wrong like what?"

"Sometimes, going back in time sends you to a slightly wrong moment," Mr. Tick explains. "A day or two past the desired date. If that happens, you will need to find Mrs. Tock to help you out."

"And she will believe me?"

"Of course she will. Who else will know about her address?" Mr. Tick says.

"I understand." I swallow the pill. "Now what?"

"Now, my dear Alice" — Mr. Tick stands up, combing his hairies — "we need to agree on the date you need to go back to."

This is the moment I have been waiting for. I need to go back a day or two before the bus accident, so I can save Jack and maybe know why I killed anyone. "A day before the bus accident."

"You think this is the time you'd have known the whereabouts of the keys?" Mrs. Tock asks skeptically.

"I can't think of a better day," I explain. "It's supposed to be the last time I remembered who I really was. Right after the accident, I was caught and sent to the asylum. I couldn't remember what happened. So the day before the bus, I must have had an accurate memory of where I hid the keys."

"What do you think, Mrs. Tock?" Mr. Tick says.

"It's her life, Mr. Tick. She wouldn't risk it for nothing."
***

As the couple prepare for my time travel, Fabiola asks to have a word with me outside.

"I'm going to make it brief," she says. "I just want to tell you that it's okay if you're not the Real Alice. You've done brave things so far. It doesn't really matter what your name is. It matters who you are."

Fabiola seems too emotional. I think she is worried she will never see me again. She is worried that the Pillar picked up a mad girl from an asylum, fooled her into being a hero, and got great results. Except that this poor girl is now about to die.

I know that because I am thinking all kinds of thoughts. I hug Fabiola and tell her the one thing I believe is true: "Don't worry, Fabiola. I don't know if I'll make it back. But I know I'm the Real Alice."

It puzzles me that suddenly Fabiola looks like she doesn't believe I'm the Real Alice.

# Chapter 46

The Queen of Hearts was enjoying her new rocking chair, made of bamboo and specially delivered to her from the African deserts by one of her mad alliances on the continent. A mad ruler who killed his people for disrespecting the religion he made up. The Queen loved this kind of madness.

But the rocking chair also reminded her of time. Rocking back and forth in a steady beat was like the ticks and tocks of a clock.

"How is my flamingo doing?" she asked her guards.

"Very well," one of the guards answered. "Dr. Tom Truckle is taking the bait."

"I knew my plan would work," she said. "How about Alice?"

"The Duchess just called in," the guard answered. "She said the plan is going well. Alice went to the future, was about to die, and now she's being forced to go back in time to find the key and, if possible, her Wonder."

"Alice has no Wonder in the past," the Queen said. "She has no idea what she is getting herself into. Once she finds the keys, she will find no solace but the address they've given her. Mrs. Tock's address. That's when she will be forced to give her the keys, which Mrs. Tock will deliver to Margaret."

"Indeed, My Queen," the guard said. "If you don't mind, the Duchess wanted me to remind you about her thing. The thing you promised to give back."

"Understood." The Queen left her chair, walking toward her phone. "I will take care of this later. Now you're dismissed. Move or I'll chop off some heads."

She waited until she was all alone in her chamber, and then dialed a forty-two-digit number on her phone.

A few breaths later, someone picked up.

"Yes?" the hollow voice said on the other side.

"All is good," the Queen said. "Alice is on her way to the past."

"And?"

"This is going to be epic," the Queen said. "It's the moment we've been waiting for. The most important moment in Wonderlanders' lives since the Circus."

"Only if she is the Real Alice," the voice said.

"Only if she is," the Queen said. "And it's so exciting."

# Chapter 47

## *Back in Time*

A long darkness veils over my soul before I can even open my eyes. In my heart, I already know I'm back in time. It's as if I can smell it. I wonder why a gut feeling doesn't want me to open my eyes.

I'm lying on my back, on a thin mattress, probably directly on the floor. The place around me stinks. The rotten smell is familiar. Something about this past is terribly wrong.

Where am I?

I imagined myself waking up in a bed in my foster family's house, still living a normal life, waiting for a phone call from Jack, maybe.

But this isn't it. I need to open my eyes now.

But before I do, there is a knock on my door.

"Open *za* door!"

This can't be. It's Waltraud Wagner.

"Time to visit *yor* doctor."

What? When?

My eyes fling open. I'm back in my cell in Radcliffe Asylum. The same cell I've been in for two years. The Tiger Lily in the pot bends over in the corner, the walls are stained with green grease, and the steel door shakes to Waltraud's rapping.

I hear the rattling of keys. She is about to open the door.

"Waltraud?" I sit up.

The vicious warden stands before me, rapping her baton on her fatty hands. She tilts her head and grimaces at me. It's as if she is surprised to see me, too.

"What am I doing here?"

"You're on vacation, honey." She cracks a laugh.

"A vacation?"

"From your mind." She loops the baton next to her ears then laughs some more. "Soon enough you'll learn the rules. I advise you to make up your mind now."

"Make up my mind about what?"

"Do you want to be electrified in the Mush Room, or would you prefer the Lullaby pill?"

I am speechless. Something is wrong. Not just with the timing. All of this doesn't add up.

"And before you attempt an escape," Waltraud says, "always know you're underground. It's really hard to escape."

"Waltraud!" I say. "What's going on?"

"This is the second time you've called me by my name." Waltraud stands back. "How do you know my name?"

"What do you mean how? You've been torturing me in the Mush Room for the past two years."

"Oh, Lord." She cups a hand on her mouth. "You're like they said. A loon multiplied by infinity." She lowers her head and taps her baton on my shoulder. "I've never seen you before, little girl. This is your first day in the asylum."

# Chapter 48

## *THE PAST: RADCLIFFE ASYLUM, OXFORD*

Waltraud pulls me by my hair. She drags me outside into the hallway I've seen a thousand times before.

Same old story. Same old torture. And same old madness.

Only it's a different time. This is what Mrs. Tock warned me of. I've returned to a day after the accident.

"Where are you taking me?" I ask her, unable to figure out what to do next. I'm in a vicious loop. In the past, but at a time when my memories are no different from the present. I can't possibly know where the keys are. Nor do I know why I killed everyone on the bus.

Back to square one. Welcome to hell all over again. My first day in the asylum. Am I going to relive the two worst years of my life?

"The doctor needs to see you," Waltraud says. "He has to access the fresh loons and advise the proper treatment."

"Dr. Tom Truckle, you mean?"

Now she pulls me harder, a little distressed. "Who are you, girl? You know too much about this asylum. You've been here before?"

"Yes."

"I never saw you. When?"

"I come from the future."

Waltraud glares at me then bursts out laughing. "Hilarious. I'm going to have so much fun with you."

"You have to believe me," I say. "I know about you. About Ogier."

"Ogier?"

"The other warden."

"I asked for another warden to help me, but they haven't sent one yet."

"See? I know things. His name is going to be Thomas Ogier. Bald. Tall. And Dumb."

"What else do you know?" Waltraud stops and pushes me against the wall.

"I know about Tom Truckle's pills. His terrible family. About the VIP ward upstairs. I know about the Mushroomers. Isn't that what you like to call the mad in here?" I take a breath. Waltraud's eyes scan me feverishly. "I'm not mad. I was here before. You have to let me go."

"That's what it's about, then," Waltraud says. "You figured out a few things about this place, maybe one of the Mushroomers told you, so I'd believe your silly time-travel story and let you go?"

"No, you don't understand. I need to leave. I need to find my Wonder."

"I will wonder you to death in the Mush Room, darling."

"Please."

"Not in a million years." She drags me across the floor again. "I think it's the pill that did this to you."

"The pill?"

"I was against giving you the pill this morning," Waltraud mumbles. "I told them it's too soon. They didn't believe me."

"What are you talking about?"

"Its effect will wither away within an hour," Waltraud says. "Until then, I'll have my fun with you."

Think, Alice. Think.

I can't let this keep going. I need to escape the asylum now. I need to find Mrs. Tock, so we can correct the path. This isn't right. If Waltraud puts me back into my cell, I won't be able to get out before twenty-four hours. I will die the worst death, in a time that isn't mine, in a cell I left some time ago.

I take a deep breath and kick Waltraud in her most delicate place.

She drops down on her knees, her face reddening with pain. Her cheeks turn into gum bubbles that are about to explode. I wriggle my hair out of her hands, but she grips a handful as I run away.

Panting and writing, I remind myself of the whereabouts of the main door. All I have to do is run. Kick some guards — although I have no None Fu in me now — and then get upstairs and out. I can't stay in here.

The first guard attacks me, but I slash my arm at his weapon, throwing him off balance. I pick up the gun and fire at him.

I didn't need to do that. What's going on with me?

The Mushroomers go wild, rapping at their steel bars in their cells. "Alice. Mad Alice!"

The next guard stands before me, hesitant to shoot back. The fear in his eyes is perplexing. Was he so scared of me when I first arrived?

"Put your gun down, or I'll shoot," I say.

Surprisingly, he cooperates. "Please don't kill me," he says. "I'll open the door leading upstairs for you."

This is too easy. What's the catch?

"Move." I point my weapon. "Tell the others to open the gate upstairs. I want a car I can drive right away."

"But of course."

I feel like a commando, a fearless warrior, but it still doesn't make sense, the way he's scared of me.

The guards open the door for me, then lie flat on their stomachs, as if I am robbing a bank, hands behind their heads.

I step up to climb the stairs the moment when my greatest weakness attacks me. The one weakness that always messed with my escaping plans. I remember the one thing that matters to me the most.

This sucks. Now I have to go back to my cell, willingly. Because I can't leave my Tiger Lily behind. Now I know what it means to me.

# Chapter 49

Running back with a rifle in my hand, I convince myself I can do it. All I have to do is pick up the Tiger Lily, use the rifle on my way back, and get out of here.

I enter the cell, hug the plant with one hand, and remember the sight of my children in the future. Tiger's boyish logic, his leadership at such a young age. Lily's incredible innocence that would make her another version of Alice in Wonderland.

A tear rolls down my cheek. This time-traveling thing is a heart-wrenching journey. I understand the wisdom of not knowing the future now. If we do, we're doomed by the curse of knowing.

I step outside, my rifle pointed out.

The guards are still on the floor. This should work. I will find Mrs. Tock and she will correct the path. I will save Jack, find the keys, and hopefully find my Wonder.

This is going to be all right, I tell myself. What more surprises could happen? I can't think of any.

But I am wrong.

A firing burst of pain rushes through my knees, so painful I drop the pot on the floor. The image of my children cracking to pieces like china dolls almost kills me right away.

I fall to one knee, dropping the rifle. Then the other knee, which I can't feel anymore. My body heats up from my toes to the back of my neck.

On my knees, I see Waltraud sneering at me. She has hit me with her baton, right in my knees, and now I can't even move.

I fall on my face, unable to comprehend what's happening to me. I needed to escape to find Mrs. Tock. Now, I won't be able to move. Now... oh, God. Now, I'm paralyzed.

The nightmare.

# Chapter 50

"What's happening to her?" Fabiola yelled at the time couple. Alice, lying on the bed, was in great pain. Her hands were trembling, and her knees were twitching.

"Relax, White Queen." Mrs. Tock was manicuring her fingernails. She seemed satisfied with the red color, now that she blew air onto it. "Pain comes with time travel."

"Pain is very interesting," Mr. Tick said, chin up, smoking a pipe. "But you should tell her what's really going on, Mrs. Tock. We're all in this together now."

"What is she supposed to tell me?" Fabiola said.

Mrs. Tock sighed. She stopped breathing on her nails and said, "I can see what's happening to her exactly."

"What?" Fabiola said. "How?"

"It's some form of telepathy," Mrs. Tock explained. "I can't contact her, though. I can only see, sometimes vaguely, where she's at and what's happening in her journey."

"A most interesting talent, Mrs. Tock," Mr. Tick commented. "Proud to be married to someone like you."

"Thank you, Mr. Tick."

"Shut up, creeps." Fabiola reached for her Vorpal sword. "Tell me what you see. What's happening to her?"

"She woke up in the wrong time," Mrs. Tock explained. "A day after she killed her classmates."

"Poor Alice." Fabiola closed her eyes, her mouth clenched before she took a deep breath to calm herself down. "How can this be fixed?"

"She will have to find me with the address I've given here. That's all," Mrs. Tock said. "See? We're not bad people."

"Always misunderstood, Mrs. Tock," Mr. Tick added.

"However, she has a little obstacle to solve," Mrs. Tock said. "Someone has knocked out her knees."

"Are you joking?"

"Not at all. Alice may be paralyzed from the knees down now," Mrs. Tock said flatly. "But I'm sure she'll find a way out."

"You obnoxious little troll." Fabiola raised her sword.

"She called me a troll." Mrs. Tock snickered, then mustered a serious face immediately. "Don't worry, White Queen. Alice's broken knees are the least of her troubles, trust me."

"Then what is?" Fabiola asked.

"She will wake up in another room now. She will meet a very important man. And she will have to deal with a big revelation, I believe."

# Chapter 51

## THE PAST: RADCLIFFE ASYLUM, OXFORD

I wake up in the room that scares me the most. A room I suspected was a figment of my imagination. A room where I am a cripple. Where a psychiatrist tells me I am mad. That there is no hope for my recovery but falling deeper into the rabbit hole of my madness.

My knees are numb. I can't feel them. I can't move. This feels so real, even in the past. I am not imagining this. Being crippled in this darkened room has always been my reality. I just never knew the circumstances that led to it.

Now it's clear to me. Waltraud broke my knees while I tried to escape the first day I arrived in the asylum. And that's when I met the faceless doctor behind the curtain of darkness separating us now.

"Welcome, Alice," he says. I can't see him. I can only smell the tobacco he's smoking from a pipe. "It's been a long time since we last met."

As he speaks, I realize I'm not under the Lullaby pill's influence now. My mind reels with memories. A lot of them now. I think I know who I am. I think I know what happened. But it can't be true. It just can't be.

Better listen to what the doctor has to say.

"I think the Lullaby pill was an early call," he says. "I should have waited a little longer."

"Why? What are you talking about?"

"I understand if you don't remember correctly. I also understand if your memories seem a little shuffled. Fact and fiction will meld into each other. But it will only take a few moments before you remember."

"Remember what?" The headache is killing me once. The memories twice.

"Remember who you really are." He slightly rocks in his chair. He seems satisfied with this conversation.

"Who in the world am I?" I tilt my head and stare into the darkness he is hiding behind. Imagine you stare into a mirror and all you see is black. "Answer me!"

"Who do you think you are?"

Playing games again. The tobacco smells like the Pillar's smoke. I know that much now. Is that possible? "Who am I?" My voice is weakening. I don't want to start sobbing. Everyone deserves to know who they are.

"You are who think you are?" he repeats.

"What's this supposed to mean? Are you saying I'm not the Real Alice?"

"On the contrary," the voice says. "You're the Real Alice. Always was. Always will be. And that may be the problem."

I dismiss his last sentence. I feel healthier in my body all of a sudden, because he said I'm the Real Alice. It's all that mattered to me from the beginning.

"Say it again, please."

He laughs. "You're the Real Alice. Don't doubt that."

"And you are?" I squint at the darkness. "It's you, the Pillar, right? For some nonsensical reason you played this game with me. Maybe you wanted to make sure I was up to the mission of saving lives. Right? Please tell me I'm right. Tell me you're the Pillar. I won't hold grudges. Just get over with it."

The silence that follows is so profound I am aware of my beating heart. The rocking chair bends forward, just a little. Smoke drifts near my face and the voice speaks to me: "No, Alice. I'm not the Pillar. You can call me Mr. Jay."

# Chapter 52

## THE PRESENT: TOM QUAD, OXFORD

Professor Carter Pillar sat on the bank in the middle of the empty quad. The sky was grey, the color of dull lives, and the rain fell like drops of unmet hopes from the sky.

Every student had left the university by this time. Everyone preferred to stay home on a day like this. A strange day, indeed. The Pillar didn't mind. He had been used to a certain amount of loneliness in the past. It wasn't always bad. Sometimes it helped him clear his mind.

He sat, fiddling with the watch in his hand.

Soon Fabiola would come. Soon everything would change. Soon she'd spit and shout in his face like she always did. But this time it was going to be the darkest hour for both of them. Soon it was going to be really hard to take sides in the Wonderland Wars.

Oh, how good and evil interjected in every aspect of life. Who was really good and who was bad? That should have been Hamlet's most daring question, not "to be or not to be."

In the middle of the rain, the Pillar pulled out a yellow piece of paper. With a ballpoint pen, he wrote something on it. One word. That was all it took. He folded the paper and tucked it back in his pocket, patted it a couple of times, closed his eyes, and let the rain wash over him.

He stared once more at his watch. It was time already.

The yellow paper in his pocket felt good. So good. Because the one word he'd written on it — it was all that mattered. The one word was the Pillar's Wonder.

# Chapter 53

"Why do people call you Mr. Jay?" I say. "How do I know you?"

"We've known each other for a long time, Alice," he says. "A little after the circus in Wonderland."

"You were at the Circus?"

"Not exactly. But we'll get into that later."

"Later when?"

"After the Lullaby's effect totally withers away."

"Why did you give it to me, then, when it messed with my head so much?"

"I didn't really give it to you," he says.

"Who did, then?"

"It was Waltraud who popped it down your throat." He pauses for a smoke. "But the real question is: whose idea was it to give you the pill?"

"Whose idea was it?" I realize I already know the answer. It's slowly coming back to me, like a gathering of million crows veiling my soul with darkness.

"You asked for the Lullaby pill, Alice."

"Me?"

"Yes. It was you."

"I think I remember that now," I say. The words are too heavy on my tongue. "I don't quite remember why."

"It's a bit complicated," Mr. Jay says. "I can't imagine why, too. But it was your call. And I wouldn't deny you anything you wish for, not after all you have done for me."

"For you? What have I done?"

"You killed everyone on the bus, Alice," Mr. Jay says. "You have no idea how much I'm pleased."

Slivers of memories flash before my eyes. I can see clearer now. No rabbit was driving the bus. Not even Carolus Ludovicus, w;hom I saw embarking the bus in an earlier vision while I was in Mushroomland.

It was me who killed everyone on the bus. Always me. And I loved it.

"If you hadn't killed them we'd never have a chance to win the Wonderland Wars," he says. "Of course, it's still a long shot to actually win the war and embrace the world with madness. But we'd never have the slightest of hopes if you haven't helped."

This is when I wish my bed were my coffin. I wish I'd sink deep into the dirt, deep enough to hide from the truth. "I helped you in winning the Wonderland Wars?" I remember the Reds in the future telling me they weren't going to kill me. That Mr. Jay had advised against it. It just can't be. I think I know now why I live in a Wonderland Compound in the future, and why Tom Truckle wouldn't tell me why he led the revolution, not me.

"The best help we ever had," Mr. Jay says.

"What do you mean when you say 'we'? Whom did I help? Who are you?"

The man lets out a brief chuckle, one that cuts through my veins. "Black Chess, Alice. Black Chess."

# Chapter 54

Sometimes the truth is a slow burn of continuous pain. The longer it takes to reveal, the more it cuts through. A sword's stroke is always merciful; a thousand small cuts are the real torture.

"Are you saying I'm…"

"Yes, you are, Alice," Mr. Jay says. "Once the Lullaby's effect leaves you, you will remember you're one of us."

All the tears in the world can't baptize me now.

"We've been planning the bus accident for years. It was our best plan. And, of course, only you could do it, but let's not get into why only you could do it now," Mr. Jay says. "The Real Alice whom everyone in Wonderland feared. The one and only."

"Feared?"

"Oh, girl. The heads you chopped off. The blood you shed." Mr. Jay is overly impressed. He may be my boss, but he is fascinated by me. "Carroll had a point, making everyone forget your face. This, or every Wonderlander would have spent the rest of their lives crapping in their pants, remembering you."

I'm darkness wrapped in black blood, dipped into the abyss of the deepest ocean. "So the whole search for the Real Alice wasn't to find the girl who will save the world?"

"I'm not sure what you're talking about. No one's really searching now, but they surely will in the future," Mr. Jay says. "The Inklings will gather someday. Some kind of prophecy. But they'll be too late."

"So the Inklings fear me, too?"

"Some of them do," he says. "Some of them foolishly think you can be converted. But I know you will never do that. You're Black Chess's most precious warrior."

"Why do you doubt that?"

"Let's face it, Alice. You've done things that can't be forgiven. Remember messing with Carroll's mind, splitting his self in two, and creating the Carolus part in him? It was genius."

"I did that?"

"You fed him a heavy dose of Lullaby pills, mixed with the Executioner's drugs, until the man collapsed. He collapsed so hard he made a deal with his split image to kill himself through you."

The curtains fall. I have nothing to say. The play is over. And when the curtains are draped, there will be no audience left to applaud. Because I may have killed them all.

"Let's not think about this now," he says. "I'm really curious why you wanted to take the Lullaby pills after all you've done."

This, I don't remember. If I was this dark beast of Wonderland, why'd I ask to forget what I had done later? Maybe some part of me, a small one, though, realized the gruesomeness of what I had done. A part that couldn't go on being the Real Evil Alice anymore. A part of me that longed for redemption. A part that wanted to forget through a Lullaby pill. A part of me that preferred I'd spend the rest of my life in an asylum. Better mad than being the Real Alice.

I really hope this tiny part is still inside me somewhere.

# Chapter 55

The call came while Margaret was staring at her reflection in the mirror, wondering if she was really as beautiful as she managed to fake.

"Margaret speaking."

"It's done," Carolus answered.

"Are you sure?"

"We should celebrate," he said. "She is the Real Alice. And she knows it. She is one of us."

Margaret's smile almost messed with her surgical beauty. She was advised against smiling too much and stretching out her Botox festival. But she couldn't help it. This was the moment everyone in Black Chess had waited for. This was the moment the Queen would be forced to give her back what she had taken from her.

"Of course Alice is back," she said. "One of us. No one can stop us from winning the war anymore."

No one can stop me from taking what belongs to me.

# Chapter 56

The Queen received a similar call, from the Cheshire this time.

"Margaret doesn't know I've called you," the Cheshire said. "She will try to keep the news from you, so you'll give her back what she wants."

"Don't worry about the ugly Duchess." The Queen was Caucus-racing in her chamber. A known Wonderlastic way of celebration. You run in place, expecting to win a race, only to realize you're stuck where you are because fate is chaining your feet. "Just tell me she is the Real Alice."

"She is."

"Holy Mushrooms and Wonderland Lilies!" She gasped. "It's her. All that I've been waiting for. Are you sure? I mean, is she still the nasty, unforgiving, ruthless girl we've always known?"

"Too soon to tell. But Mrs. Tock confirmed what she saw in the past. She even saw her meeting with Mr. Jay."

"Then it's her. Damn you, Lewis, for erasing her image from our minds. We could have found her earlier. Tell me, Cheshire, how is she taking it?"

"Mrs. Tock says the girl is pretty shocked. There is still that small part of her that wishes she could redeem herself, but I think it's too small to have an effect on her when she comes back to the present."

"I wouldn't dismiss this part." The Queen rubbed her chin. "From what I understand now, she asked for the pill after the bus accident. She does have that goodie-goodie part in her. It must be suppressed."

"I believe this is what she did," the Cheshire said. "Mrs. Tock believes Alice took incredible doses of Lullaby pills so she'd forget who she is."

"We'll know the rest of the truth eventually," the Queen said. "Now, you have to make sure Mrs. Tock and Mr. Tick bring her back."

"It won't be easy, as she still has to find her Wonder to return."

The Queen went silent. Margaret's plan wasn't perfect after all. They had dug a hole for themselves by tricking Alice into needing her Wonder to survive. "I don't care," she said. "I want my Real Alice back. I need her so we win the war. Fix it."

"I'll see what we can do. How about the keys?"

"She is the Real Alice. She will find them. All that matters is bringing her back now!"

The Queen hung up and then paced left and right, her dogs following her everywhere. "Think. Think. Think," she told herself, knowing that thinking wasn't her best talent. "Guards!"

A few of them arrived immediately.

"I want you to chop off the heads of a thousand lions," she ordered. "Find them. Buy them. Chop them off. This is the most festive day of my life. Understood?"

"Where do we find the lions, My Queen?" a guard asked.

"You find the lions where everyone finds the lions."

"Which is where, exactly?" the guard asked.

"Stupid guards." The Queen jumped atop a chair and yelled at him, "Did you ever see a lion?"

"Yes."

"Where?"

"On TV."

"That's why you don't know where lions are. This is what TV does to you, younger generation. Now go chop off the heads of a thousand lions."

The guard shrugged. "I'm sorry, My Queen. But where do I find the lions, again?"

The Queen stamped her feet, risking the unbalancing of the chair. "Where lions always are. The cages of a zoo. Don't you know that they like to live in cages and have people watching them all the time?"

"Of course, My Queen," the puzzled guards said, and left the room.

The Queen began itching her chin. "What will I do with Alice when she comes back?" She jumped off the chair and talked to her dogs, whose ears stood erect. "I'm sure she will help us win the war. But if there is still that nagging part in her longing for redemption, what should I do with her? I need to protect myself."

She paced more and more. Swallowed a few nuts. Choked on one. Spat it out, and a dog caught it. "Damn you, Pillar." The Queen halted in the middle of her chamber. "That's why you got into the asylum, you devious butterfly. You knew it was her. You wanted to convert her against us." She walked to her balcony for a fresher breath of air. "I think I'll have to find a way to keep the Real Alice away after I use her to win the war."

And then the Queen had an idea. "What about a compound? The Wonderland Compound. Where all those who help me win the war will enjoy immunity against the madness in the world." She clicked her fingers and jumped atop the balcony's rail. "I'm a genius. Alice, like any other girl, will want to get married and have kids. I'll get a boy to seduce her, impregnate her, and then she will be knee-deep in her personal troubles. I'll offer her a lavish life in the compound. A life she will never refuse. What a plan!"

# Chapter 57

## *THE PRESENT: TOM QUAD*

Fabiola arrived on time, shivering underneath a black umbrella. The rain was still pouring. The Pillar stood up. He felt for her. The tension in her eyes told him she knew. There was no going back now.

"Does it make a difference if I tell you I hate you again?" she said.

"Hating someone never makes a difference," the Pillar said. "Loving someone does."

"Shut up, or I'll stab you with my Vorpal sword."

"I know you're capable of that, and even worse," the Pillar said. "I just don't know why you haven't stabbed me yet."

"Why, Carter?" she pleaded. "Why did you wake her up? She had chosen to stay mad and save the world from her wrath."

"Everyone deserves a second chance."

"Don't feed me your lies, not after all that you have done in the past."

"Everyone deserves a second chance," the Pillar said again. His tone the same. He wanted to pass a message. Sometimes you had to tell people twice to get them out of their heads.

"She is beyond redemption."

"Says the White Queen who killed millions and resorted to becoming a nun?"

"I killed in the name of glory." She gritted her teeth. "I killed to save children from Wonderland Monsters. I killed for the Inklings, not Black Chess. For a good cause."

"So says the religious bomber who explodes a school bus full of kids every day. We can justify all we want. The truth will remain blurry, and we can only trust our hearts."

"So that's it? You believed in your heart when you woke the dark Alice up, made a paper-thin hero out of her."

"Yes, Fabiola. All you have to do is look at her. Just look without prejudice. She can do it."

"Do what?" Fabiola asked. "Don't you remember what she did after the Circus?"

"Funny how were remember what she did, but don't remember her."

"Stop messing with my mind. She went bonkers. The darkest Wonderland Monster of all."

"You're talking about the circus, which you helped her to find in the vision when she was in the Garden of Cosmic Speculation."

"I did it to prove she wasn't the Real Alice."

"Liar," the Pillar said. "You did it to prove she *was* the Real Alice, so you could kill her. Or you did it because you believed in this delusional girl who had magically saved so many lives in so few weeks."

Fabiola shrugged, drops of rain splashing on her nose. "And you fooled us all. You fed us all these lies about her being a hero."

"I fed you the truth, one lie after the other. Sometimes good comes out of evil. It is about to get dark in a few hours." He nodded at the skyline. "It doesn't mean the sun won't shine tomorrow."

"You're twisting the words to your liking, like you always have, Carter. Do you have any idea how much damage you caused to her by waking her up?"

"Damage to her, or to you?"

"Stop twisting my words, I said. What was the point, Carter? What was the point of proving she was the Real Alice?"

"To show you she can do good," the Pillar said. "To show she can save the world from the Cheshire, the Muffin Man, the Executioner, Carolus, and even me."

"She did it thinking she was someone else. Someone you made her think she is."

"So the things we do knowing who we really are count, and the things we do pretending we're a better someone else don't?"

"Oh, spare me the philosophy."

"Or spare you the truth?"

"The truth is she is a killer, Black Chess's favorite."

"The truth is she is a lifesaver who stood in Black Chess's way many times," the Pillar countered. "Even the timeline suggests what I'm saying is true. Once she was evil, now she is a hero. Let it go."

"You're trying to fix a broken soul because you can't fix yourself."

"I'm immune to insults, Fabiola. Try something else."

"You want something else?" She stepped forward, locking eyes with him. It was the moment he feared the most. But it was inevitable. "From this day on, you and your precious little devil are the Inklings' enemies. My enemies."

The Pillar shrugged.

"I will declare war on Alice."

"I knew you would."

"That's because you know me from way back. You know who I really am. The fierce warrior that fought for the Inklings no matter what. Winning the Wonderland War is the greater cause. Not the redemption of your little mad princess."

"Just don't tell it to her in the face," the Pillar said. "She really loves you. It will crush her."

Fabiola's face twitched. She had just confessed her love for Alice a few hours back. Now, in the blink of an eye, the tables had turned. But the Pillar knew Fabiola wouldn't give in. She'd had a rough childhood herself. And every Wonderlander counted on her.

"Try to forgive and look ahead, Fabiola," the Pillar said. "Even Lewis bought into my plan."

"Which really puzzles me," she said. "Every time I remember him hugging and advising her in the Tom Tower, or when his apparition appeared to her in the Inklings, telling her she was the hero, my mind reels."

"It wasn't easy for him," the Pillar said. "When I tried to take the Lullaby pill from him in the future, he wouldn't let me."

"That's because in the future he regretted letting you help her," Fabiola said. "Come on, Pillar. Open your eyes. Can't you see we lost the war in the future? Doesn't that tell you that backing her up isn't the right thing to do?"

The Pillar said nothing. He lifted one arm and tapped his left breast pocket. His yellow note hiding inside. "I have my reasons."

"Stubborn as you always have been." She sighed. "One of the reasons I could never love you."

"Could is good. It means you wanted to but didn't."

"Listen to me," she said. "Alice is now in the past, realizing who she really is. It's either she finds her way back through that Wonder, or whatever that is, or she dies."

"She won't die."

"Just listen." Her knuckles whitened around the umbrella. "If she dies, then it's all good. I can lead the Inklings to win the war against Black Chess. If she finds her Wonder and lives..."

"What happens then, Fabiola?"

"I will kill you both," she said without flinching. He knew she meant it. And it complicated things.

The Pillar watched her walk away, almost disappearing behind the rain. "Fabiola!" he called after her.

"What now, Carter?" She stopped, but didn't turn around.

"There is only one way to kill her."

"What's that?"

"You will have to kill me first."

# Chapter 58

Waltraud wheels me back to my cell. I stare at my immobile legs in dismay. I'm sweating out of shock. But I am not crying anymore. I've dried all my tears already.

"Mr. Jay wants you to rethink the Lullaby pill," Waltraud says, sending me into my cell.

Speechless, I stare into the mirror in front of me. I've witnessed this scene before, only I thought I was hallucinating. I thought I was dreaming. I thought I was mad. Turns out I'm not. I'm reliving my past in full color.

How I wish I was mad right now.

"There is no rabbit in the mirror," I manage to say.

"There's never been a rabbit," Waltraud says. She whispers in my ear, "It's always been you. We're proud of you."

I let out a chuckle. A painful one. A mixture of laughter and crying. Pain and pleasure. Sanity and insanity.

It occurs to me that I'm just confused. If this is my past, why am I sad? I am the Real Alice. A dark and vicious one that everyone was looking for because they feared me the most.

Why am I sad, then? I can't escape me. Why is there a nagging part of me wanting me to be a hero?

"I'm really sorry I broke your knees," Waltraud says. The irony. "You were under the pill's influence. I had to stop you from escaping. I'm really sorry."

When I raise my eyes to meet hers in the mirror, I realize she is scared of me. Now that the pill's influence has worn off, she is expecting me to return to my real self. She thinks I will hurt her.

"I hope you don't hold grudges against me," she says. "Please don't hurt me."

The irony, times two. Or better, times Walraud's weight. Even better, times the number of times she will fry me in the Mush Room in the future.

"Do you want me to wash your feet?" she offers. "Mr. Jay says it's going to take you six months for your knees to recover."

"No, Waltraud. I don't want you to wash my feet. I want to ask you about Dr. Tom Truckle."

"The pill-popping fool who thinks he is building an ark and saving the Mushroomers to win the Wonderland Wars?" Her whole body shakes when she laughs.

"So he doesn't know about me?"

"We let him pursue his plan with Carroll's legacy," Waltraud says. "I pretend I fear him the most when he talks to me, just to keep up the act. But he's a pawn in Black Chess's plan."

This explains a lot about him in the future. The poor man is chasing a loom of nothingness. But I don't want Waltraud to sense my sympathy. I'm not sure why my inner self resists being the Bad Alice, but it's how I feel.

Maybe it's because of what the Pillar showed me in the future. Maybe it's been the Pillar's plan from the beginning: to show me the good person I can become in the future, preparing me for a hard choice when I learn who I really am in the past.

My head isn't clear yet, and for whatever reason, I need to play along. "Good. It's best to keep Dr. Truckle in the dark."

Waltraud's smile broadens. "Does that mean you're not taking the pill? Does that mean you'll stay one of us?"

"I haven't decided yet. Not before I meet the Queen of Hearts. I need to ask her something."

"Of course," she says. "I will call her right away."

And now the Queen is in the palm of my hand. I own her because I'm Black Chess's favorite. Who would have thought?

# Chapter 59

"What can I do for you, dear Alice?" the Queen of Hearts says, standing before me.

She hasn't possessed the Queen of England's body yet at this point. She looks as ugly as I've seen her in Wonderland. Stocky, short, her facial features almost unrecognizable. Like a frog, with bulging eyes, a lost nose, and a big mouth.

"Still as ugly as you've always been," I mock her, testing my credibility.

"Thanks for the compliment." She lowers her head, fidgeting with her hands. "I'm working on a new face in this world. Haven't found a spell to get it, though."

"How about Margaret?"

"She was the first one to arrive from Wonderland. She had someone surgically fix her. But she's taller than me, so it's easier for her. She's in Parliament right now."

"Proud of her," I say. "She isn't wasting time playing by the book."

"I'll tell her that. She'll be happy." She stops to think about it. "But maybe I shouldn't tell her about you now. You know no one knows about you but me and Mr. Jay."

I didn't know that. It explains why none of the Wonderlanders knows about the sequence of the events in the future. I wonder how the Queen didn't recognize me in the future, then. I'm sure I will know how along the way. "How about Waltraud? She knows who I am."

"Don't worry about that loser," the Queen says. Waltraud isn't in the room. "We're feeding her a huge dose of Lullaby pills right now. She will not remember you. I believe that's your wish, right?" She raises her eyes to meet mine. "I understand you don't want to take the pill and spend the rest of life in the asylum."

I nod, wanting her to spill the rest for me. Why did the Bad Alice want to forget about what she had done? It can't be that I changed overnight. There must be a reason. I have to find out why.

"Mr. Jay told me about the deal. If you take the pill, we will have to take it, too," the Queen says. "You don't want us to remember you as well."

So that's why no one remembers me in the future. The Bad Alice had a change of heart and ordered her obituary, spending the rest of her life in an asylum.

"I'm impressed your stupid brain managed to fully understand my wishes," I say, playing my part.

The Queen's face twitches. She fears me, but she holds grudges. It makes sense. She once ruled Wonderland with her stupidity and anger. Then something happened after the circus. Who knows what? It's hard to bring the subject to the table right now. "Do you happen to also remember why I need the pill?" I say. "I need to make sure you understand."

"Of course," she says. "Because of Jack. I'm really sorry."

"What about Jack?"

"But you know why, dear Alice."

"Just spit it out."

"You regret having accidentally killed Jack on the bus," she says. "Even though everyone on this bus had to die, Jack wasn't meant to be on it. He didn't have to die. I understand how this changed you. Love changes everything."

# Chapter 60

Now that I know what changed my dark heart, I tell the Queen she and Mr. Jay have to take the pill when I take it. I tell her that I'm still determined to forget and spend the rest of my life in the asylum.

The Queen complies, and confirms Mr. Jay has taken the pill. I only ask her to watch the sunset outside for one last time before I resort to my madness inside the dark asylum. The Queen complies, and now we're outside in her limousine, driving around.

"You can still forget about the pill," the Queen, sitting next to me, advises. "You can rule the world when we win the war. I have information that someone has found a way to bring the Wonderland Monsters into this world. Week by week they will arrive and wreak havoc on this world until we take our revenge on humans."

I let her talk, not paying attention. I know the rest already. I even know the parts she doesn't, like the Pillar helping me out of my dark world and turning me into a hero.

I am taking a deep breath. I will need it. I have a big plan ahead of me. I need to focus.

I have a handful of Lullaby pills hidden in my fist. When the limousine stops at an intersection, I pull them out and stuff them into the Queen's mouth, choking her long enough until she swallows them all.

The driver tries his luck at fighting me. I twist his head with my hands, and he ends up staring backward at the comatose — and now amnesiac — Queen of Hearts. "I need you to drive me somewhere," I tell him. "Or I'll never fix your head."

"I'll do what you want," he says. "Please, Alice. Don't kill me."

I turn his head back. It doesn't fit exactly — it's a little skewed at the cheeks — but he is glad he is alive.

"Thank you," he says. "Where to?"

The million-dollar question. I focus hard, trying to remember Mrs. Tock's address, the one she gave me through the pink pill in the Inklings. I think the Lullaby pill I took in the past messed with pill I took in the present where I came from.

Remember it, Alice. Come on!

As we chug through the streets of Oxford, I can't remember the address. Maybe I've been exposed to too much emotional stress. I should remember it.

We kick the Queen out on the street. The driver puts her in a garbage can, telling me he loathed her and would do anything for me.

When he comes back, we drive left and right, everywhere, hoping the buildings will make me remember, hand me a clue.

Where does Mrs. Tock live now?

Then it comes to me. I'm not just in the wrong area. I'm in the wrong city. Mrs. Tock's address is in London.

"London it is," the driver says.

"I will need my wheelchair first," I remind him — also reminding myself that I am a cripple.

"It's fixed on top of the car. Don't worry."

"And I will need you to help me up a few stories in London. Got that?"

"I will do what you ask for," he says. "May I ask where I will be lifting you up?"

"A hidden room in the Big Ben tower."

# Chapter 61

Mr. Tick and Mrs. Tock live in a hidden room in the Big Ben. It has a wall for a door that only opens when you knock on it six times, like a secret cave. They live in a lavish, huge room inside. The only disadvantage is the horribly loud sound each time the Big Ben strikes.

But being married since the beginning to time, both of them aren't bothered by it. In fact, they look so bored, they love it when it bangs.

Mr. Tick is certainly bored of his ticks. I watch him blame Mrs. Tock for being a boring wife who can't find a way for him to spice up his life. Mr. Tick really hates London. He hates the rainy weather, the drunks late at night, the football games, and calls it a boring city. Mrs. Tock keeps telling him that soon the Wonderland Monsters will arrive, and the city will become incredibly entertaining. Mr. Tick says it's all lies, like there's never been a real Severus Snape in Harry Potter.

The couple are so bored that Mrs. Tock doesn't mind finding me in her kitchen. She doesn't ask how I got inside their secret hideout. Worse, she doesn't remember who I am.

This is going to take some time.

"Tea?" she offers me.

"Please." I am trying to think of the right words to explain to her that I am from the future and that she is supposed to help me.

"I don't know how to please my husband," she complains. "I mean, our marriage was perfect the first two thousand years. The love, the cuddles, and all the things we did together. But then, a thousand years after a thousand years, things went down the drain."

"How long have you been married?"

She scratches her head. "I really forgot."

"Never mind." I wave a hand, like a good neighbor chitchatting with her. "I'm sure it's been a long time. Ever had kids?"

"Mr. Tick doesn't want to." She lowers her head. "He thinks he is still young. He still chases young girls."

"Midlife crisis." I rub my cup.

"He says I'm boring," she explains. "That I'm always late."

"You're Mrs. Tock. It's who you are."

"See? I'm meant to be late. All women are meant to be late. We need time in front of the mirror."

"I agree." Now that I can finally stare into a mirror.

"Of course, he doesn't need a mirror. First of all, he is too tall for all mirrors. Secondly, he has no hair to comb."

"Three hairies, I believe."

"I'm surprised you can see them." She snickers. "He keeps lubricating them, combing, and even dying them. All for that girl he's liked recently."

"I'll bet she is young."

"Nineteen. Can you believe it? He's easily her great-great ancestor. Her name is Lorina."

"Lorina?"

"Lorina Wonder."

I rest my case. I have nothing to say.

"Now he wants a divorce, which we're not allowed to have."

"Of course. What would the world be without a tick and a tock?"

"I'm glad you understand," she says. "He's looking for a cure for baldness these days."

"I bet he's been looking for it for a few thousand years now."

"And it's all a hoax. Can't grow back hair unless you go back in time." Mrs. Tock laughs. "So do I know you?"

I haven't told her my name. "I was sent to you from the future."

She bursts out laughing. "Nice one."

"No, really," I say. "Two years in the future you sent me back here. You gave me this address and told me you can help me when something goes wrong."

Mrs. Tock's face dims. She doesn't like what I'm saying at all.

"Listen." I am trying my best to embrace my Bad Alice personality, but it's not working. "You were supposed to send me a day back, but you messed up, and I need you to help me go back to yesterday."

"You're insane."

"Not anymore." I grin. "If you don't help me, I will die in the next few hours."

# Chapter 62

The Cheshire booked a room in the hotel after they'd told him they had a DVD player inside. In spite of being penniless, he used Jack's charm on the receptionist, a blond girl, whom he showed a card trick. One of the benefits of having access to Jack's mind — and a possible generous source of income in the future.

The Cheshire entered the room and turned on the DVD, then pushed a stolen version of *Titanic* in. People had told him *Titanic* was the cheesiest when it came to illogical portrayals of romance on film.

The Cheshire liked that. He was experiencing the same thing in Jack's head; his continuing love for Alice both annoyed and amazed the Cheshire.

An hour and a half into the movie, the Cheshire was weeping into tissues—he was glad no one was watching him.

But he couldn't help it. Love and sacrifice were new concepts to him, let alone coming from the freakin' humans.

He began regretting the way he'd earlier celebrated the Bad Alice's return with the Queen of Hearts on the phone. Of course, Alice being the Real Alice satisfied his insatiable desire to hurt humans in this world. But only if he hadn't entered Jack's body and brain.

Why did I ever possess his soul?

Now, sitting here, his tears wetting his cheeks, he didn't know whether to help Alice become a hero or resort to the evil one she had always been. It was a shame she didn't know someone like Jack loved her so much. Even the Cheshire had begun having feelings for Alice.

How he wished someone loved him this way. The last cat he'd loved back in Belgium was a fraud. She was after the delicious rat he'd just caught.

But maybe the Cheshire was destined to become Jack. Alice's lover. As weird and creepy as it was, even to him, it seemed his only way out of his pain of being a nobody.

Possessing any soul he wished didn't prove him as invincible as he'd always thought. It was time for the Cheshire to be somebody. Jack seemed like a good choice.

Besides, he had begun to fall in love with the card player.

But still, sometimes the older Cheshire rose inside and wanted to vomit all of this love out. Yuck. It was as bitter as expired milk.

The Cheshire, confused like never before, sat on the bed with one last idea in his head. The most interesting, actually. He vowed not to make a decision about Jack's love for Alice, not before he knew why Jack came back for her.

If he could only locate that part of the memory in Jack's brain.

# Chapter 63

## *The Past: Big Ben, London*

"Go away!" Mrs. Tock shrills. "Who are you? Time travel isn't possible."

"Please, Mrs. Tock," I say. "You promised to help me. How else do you think I figured out your hiding place?"

"Go away, you creepy girl in the wheelchair."

I use her fear and wheel myself after her, creeping her out. "Think of it. I know a lot of things about you. Things no one else knows."

"Like what?" She steps away from me.

"Like Mr. Tick loves tea."

"So?"

"And brownies."

"So what?"

"He never lets you near his brownies."

She stops and stares skeptically at me. "It still doesn't prove you're from the future."

"Tell you what." I squeeze her against the wall with my wheelchair. "Forget about who I am. If I make Mr. Tick love you back, will you help me?"

"Says the young, inexperienced girl in a wheelchair."

"Just humor me. Go now and stop time. He will like it."

"We've stopped time a million times. It's boring."

"Because it never occurred to you to mess with people," I say. "Stop time and push a car over the cliff. Make one woman bore into another's nose. Switch things. It'll be fun. He will like it." *Sorry, world. I have to do it.*

"You think?"

"Just do it!"

\*\*\*

I spend the next hour trying not to think about the crazy accidents happening in London when time stops. Mrs. Tock returns with a broad smile on her face. "He liked it." She jumps in place. "He even swore to forget about Lorina Wonder. Who are you, creepy girl?"

"Says the creepiest woman in history." I roll my eyes.

"What did you just say?"

"Was just coughing. So are you going to help me?"

"Only because you made my husband like me." She sits next to me and rubs her chin. "Why do you want to travel back in time?"

*So it's possible, Mrs. Tock.* "I need to go back to yesterday to save a few friends from dying."

"Every fool's wish."

"What do you mean?"

"Everyone thinks if they go back in time, they can change the future. It never works. Whatever you do, time will find a way to stay on course—a few casualties and tiny changes might occur."

Tiny changes. Like Jack staying alive? I'd like that. Also, I'd like to know what happened on the bus. "I'll take whatever time gives me."

"Time is sneaky and unreliable, I must warn you. Besides, if you're from the future like you said, you're going to die either way." She eyes me. "I see you already know that. How long do you have?"

"Ten hours. Give or take."

"Then I'd advise you to spend them messing with people's minds here. You're doomed, crippled girl."

"Unless I find my Wonder in the past."

Mrs. Tock laughs, throwing her head back. She raps on the table and addresses her husband. "Did you hear what she just said, Mr. Tick?"

"She wants to find her Wonder so she stays alive," Mr. Tick says, sipping his tea and reading tomorrow's news. A special Tick Tock edition.

"What's wrong with finding my Wonder?" I say.

"You know what that even is?" Mrs. Tock snickers.

"The one thing we do in our lives and are forever proud of—or something like that?"

"You know how long me and Mrs. Tock have been alive?" Mr. Tick says. "We've never known what our Wonder is."

That's because you're two mad morons, obsessed with the misery of others. "Leave that part to me. Just send me back in time."

"Are you sure?" Mrs. Tock says. "Sometimes it's better not to go back to yesterday." She points at the tattoo on my hand. "Sometimes it's better not to know."

"I know the worst about me already. I don't think it gets worse than that."

"Send the poor girl back, Mrs. Tock," Mr. Tick suggests. "At least she'd enjoy not being a cripple for the next few hours. Or were you a cripple yesterday, too?" he asks me.

"No, I wasn't."

"As you wish, my lovely husband." Mrs. Tock rubs her hand on my eyes. "Now close your eyes and count to seven. Can't guarantee you'll wake in heaven."

# Chapter 64

The best thing about the past is that I'm not crippled. I wake up in a bed in a room I now remember well. The room on the second floor of the house where I've spent most of my adult life with my foster family.

The sun outside is shining brightly. There are no hints of the possibility of rain or greying skies. It looks like a beautiful day — unfortunately, the day I will kill my classmates.

I take a moment in front of the mirror, admiring my seventeen-year-old look. It boggles my mind how innocent I look. If I were the Bad Alice all this time, why don't I feel like it in the past? Is it really the fact that the Pillar exposed me to the possibility of becoming a better person in the future? Do I really have a chance to rewrite my evil ways? To change the world?

I dress up for school and descend the stairs.

"Alice, darling," my mother addresses me, fixing me sandwiches in the kitchen. Either I managed to fool her into thinking I'm innocent, or I really have the power to change. "I fixed you the tuna sandwich you love."

"Thanks." I take it and then slowly say, "Mum?"

She kisses me on the cheek. "Please forgive your sisters," she says. "They're horrible. One day they will know your worth."

"Forgive them?"

"For what they did yesterday, locking you in the basement. Don't you remember?"

"Ah, that." I wonder if I should confront her with the knowledge that they're not my sisters, and that she isn't my mother. But what's the point, really?

I need to ask practical questions. "Did you see Jack?" She must know him at this point — or doesn't she know about my relationships at this time?

"What about Jack?" Lorina descends the stairs.

"I wonder where I can find him."

"Why?" She snatches my sandwich and tucks it into her bag. "Tuna. Yuck!"

"Do you know where he is or not?"

"You better stay away from Jack, Alice." Edith arrives.

"What is that supposed to mean?"

"Jack is mine," Lorina says. "All mine."

"And you've been looming for some time," Edith says.

I thought we were a couple by now.

"It boggles my mind why you think he'd be interested in you," Lorina says. "He is mine."

"Not yet," Edith reminds her.

"I always get what I want," Lorina says, chin up.

I don't have time for this nonsense.

"And what's with the thinning hair?" Edith points at my withering hair. I guess it haunts me everywhere I travel in time. I think it has something to do with the time I have left alive.

I comb my head with hands. No time to be embarrassed about it. My mother has already disappeared somewhere.

"We shouldn't lock her in the basement too often," Lorina says. "It looks like rats are ripping out her hair."

"Looks better that way," Edith says. "She looks mad. To the point."

The sisters giggle.

I need to know where to find Jack, couple or no couple. Or should I just stay away from him? If we're not a couple, why would he get on the bus with me later? I'm confused here.

"I know he's yours," I tell Lorina. "Can't you just tell me where I can find him? I need to return a pen I borrowed."

"A pen? Such a lame excuse."

Why can't I just be the Bad Alice and choke both of them right now?

"Tell you what," Edith says. "I'm suggesting you forget about school today."

"Yeah," Lorina says. "I'm seducing Jack into kissing me today. Better find something else to do."

"Like what?"

"Like your favorite mad professor at Oxford University." Edith giggles. Lorina giggles back.

"Mad professor?"

"The one whom you trust over everyone else," Lorina says. "The one you think understands you."

"Aren't you too young for him?" Edith laughs.

"Who are you talking about?"

"Don't pretend you're naive." Lorina waves her hand, dismissing me. "Go to him. Professor Carter Pillar, who believes that Wonderland exists, like you do."

I am speechless.

"Honestly, it's a joke," Edith says to Lorina. "You won't believe how many young girls attend his free lectures, escaping school. Each one of them believes she is Alice."

They both laugh and walk away.

In my mind, I think that finding the Pillar isn't a bad idea. He always has a way out in these situations. I follow them out. Going to Oxford University wouldn't be a problem.

# Chapter 65

The girls swarming outside the lecture hall are all teenagers. Most of them are certified nerds. A few pigtails here, thick glasses there, and of course they all carry an Alice in Wonderland gadget. Several goth-like girls are also present, loud talkers and jokers, wearing silver piercings and black tattoos, hair dyed in pink and dressed like rock stars, and wearing t-shirts about an evil Alice. Last but not least are the girls in costumes. All Wonderlastic masks, disguised as the Hatter, the Rabbit, and Queen of Hearts, and more.

Oxford University has turned into a simple Comic Con, waiting for Professor Carter Pillar. What can I say? It's the Pillar. Always influential and doing what he likes to celebrate madness.

I walk among them, hugging my books and strapping on my backpack. The girls talk about their crushes on the professor. His free spirit, and the fact that he understands them.

"I hope you don't end up in an asylum," I mumble, chugging through.

"You know Alice is real?" a girl suggests to her friends. "Professor Pillar says so. There is a Wonderland War coming."

I roll my eyes and stay silent. I think we're all waiting for the lecture room's door to open. There is a bulletin board that talks about the Pillar's theories on insanity. It basically spreads the idea about the world going nuts. It also promotes hookah smoking.

A few professors, wearing ties and smoking pipes, pass through the corridor. They stare at us, Wonderland believers, as if we're parasites. One of them mentions the committee's disgust with the Pillar's ways, wondering how the university permits him to gather those teenagers and poison their thoughts.

Then the doors open.

The girls compete to be first inside. I wait for the clatter to subside and follow in. The lecture hall is almost full, so I resort to a lonely bench in the last two rows, and watch the Pillar enter.

My plan is to wait for a chance to approach him and talk him into helping me with finding Jack. But my plan is thrown out of the window when I take a better look at the professor.

How could this be?

The vicious serial killer is nothing but a nerdy professor like I have seen before.

# Chapter 66

Professor Pillar wears a multicolored jacket too short at the waist. It's battered and probably hasn't been washed since Wonderland. His trousers are pink, too large, and he wears flip-flops. His eyes hide behind thick glasses with black frames. Glasses that desperately need wiping. The man stutters when he welcomes his students. He has a tic of adjusting his glasses whenever he says something. For God's sake, the Pillar blushes when a girl compliments him.

I sit, mouth agape, unable to fathom what's going on. How is this going to help me? I suppress a shriek when he mentions his idol is Indiana Jones.

I spend the lecture in a terrible kind of awe, waiting for him to finish. I need to go talk to him. Wake him up.

When he is done, all I have left is seven hours. I slither through the crowd and pull him by the arm. "Professor!"

"Yes?" He adjusts his glasses. "How may I help you, kiddo?"

"I need to talk to you."

His eyes dart sideways. "Aren't we already?"

"In private," I whisper.

His eyes widen. He blushes and worries. Says nothing.

"It's important," I whisper. "I'm Alice."

"Alice?"

"I'm the Real Alice you're looking for." I grit my teeth.

He backs away, suspiciously scanning me from head to toe. Then he slouches, hugging his book, about to leave.

"We need to talk alone." I pull him back again. "I need your help."

"Who are you?" He stops, irritated now.

It's going to be hard to explain things to him among all those girls. Then I remember seeing a poster out in the streets of the upcoming *Star Wars* movie. It gives me an idea. "I have tickets for the next *Star Wars*. Front row. Premiere day."

His eyes widen again. Immediately he excuses himself and pulls me into his office. He locks the door behind us, gets behind his desk, and glares at me. "Is Darth going to be there?"

Really? I fist one hand. Is this really happening, or is he making it up?

I rap my hand on the desk and lean forward as he slumps back in his seat. "Look, whoever the Jub Jub you are now, I'm Alice Pleasant Wonder. Mary Ann. I used to know you in Wonderland. We go back then. Not in Wonderland, but in the future. I have seven hours to save myself from dying because of a lapse in time travel. According to the *Hitchhiker's Guide to Wonderlastic Time Travels*, I need to find my Wonder or I will die. But even if I can't find it, I need to save Jack. You know Jack? In fact, I need to save my classmates, probably the hordes of girls outside, from killing them in a bus accident a few hours from now. I need you to stop me from doing that. No, this isn't right. I need you to help me stop me from killing my classmates and ending up in an asylum for the next two years. Do. You. Get. That?"

The Pillar sinks deeper into this chair, shielding his face with his arms. The look on his face is priceless. He stares at me and says, "Is the hookah you're smoking that good?"

# Chapter 67

"What's going on with her?" Fabiola said. "What's happening to Alice?"

"Not good," Mr. Tick said, reading the paper, some unearthly publication called *Newsweek*. No, it was actually called *Nextweek*. "Tell her, Mrs. Tock."

"Alice can't find Jack," Mrs. Tock explained.

"So?" Fabiola said.

"She can't save him."

"I don't care about Jack. What about her Wonder?"

"Well, she can't find that either." Mrs. Tock seemed worried. Unlike earlier when she had all the fun, now she knew if Alice died, they couldn't get the keys.

"Good," Fabiola said.

"Good?"

"As long as she can't find her Wonder, she will die in the past." Fabiola sat down, relieved.

"Really?" Mrs. Tock said. "You want her to die?"

"The Real Alice must die."

"I thought you loved her," Mrs. Tock said. "You've repeatedly helped her fight monsters."

"Thinking she was a regular girl doing good in the world."

"And letting her think she is Alice?"

"We're all delusional." Fabiola didn't mind her blunt deflations. "If it serves the good cause, so be it."

"And now you want her to die in her past, even though you know she may change and become good in the future? Aren't humans always redeemable? What about absolution?"

"Don't feed me the words I fed the world when I was in the Vatican," Fabiola said. "Evil has to be cut from its roots."

"Well, she still has a chance to live," Mrs. Tock teased her.

"How so?" Fabiola stood up.

"She found the Pillar."

"The Pillar? The day of the accident?"

"Yes."

"The Pillar was useless that day," Fabiola said. "His memory was wiped out a year earlier at the time."

"Is that so?" Mr. Tick lowered his newspaper. "I don't quite remember it, Mrs. Tock."

"That's because we've got a lot of things to remember. Hundreds of thousands of years of memory mess up our memories."

"What happened to him?" Mr. Tick scratched his cantaloupe head.

"I think someone secretly fed him a string of Lullaby pills to put him to rest." Mrs. Tock scratched her head as well, hoping to *scratch* a memory out of it. "I wonder who."

"Maybe if you scratch my head you will remember," Mr. Tick offered.

"Thanks, dear husband, for allowing me to scratch your head," Mrs. Tock said. "But I'm afraid if I scratch it you'd lose one of your hairies, and blame it on me."

"Wise woman," Mr. Tick said. "Remind me again, why did I marry you?"

"That was a long time ago." She sighed. "I don't even remember when."

"Not even me," he said. "But I think I remember a big bang rocking this world that day."

"That'd be our wedding bells, Mr. Tick." Mrs. Tock patted him, turning back to Fabiola. "So anyways, even though Alice found the Pillar, she can't make it, right?"

"I don't think so," Fabiola said. "At this point the Pillar hardly remembered anything."

"I'm disappointed. I really wanted to see the Real Alice live," Mrs. Tock said. "I still can't understand who was able to fool the Pillar into swallowing Lullaby pills. This has to be someone as devious as devils."

"It was me," Fabiola said. "I had to do it."

# Chapter 68

## THE PAST: OXFORD UNIVERSITY

For a whole hour I keep pushing the Pillar to the edges. Until something happens. A headache so severe he drops to the floor, just like Lewis Carroll did a million times. I wonder if this is the moment when another Carolus surfaces out of the Pillar.

But it doesn't happen that way.

"I think I remember something. But I'm not sure what."

"I can help you remember more." I help him stand up. "Does Fabiola ring a bell?"

"The nun from the Vatican?"

"The White Queen, actually."

"Don't be silly," the Pillar says. "Next thing you'll tell me the Queen of England is the Queen of Hearts."

"It hasn't happened yet, but yes, she will be."

The Pillar stops then ruffles his hair. He hasn't yet acquired a hat at this point.

"How about you will kill twelve people in the next two years?"

He laughs, adjust his glasses, and says, "Me?" He raises an eyebrow. "I don't even know how to use a gun."

"Of course you do. Someone has wiped out your memory or something. I can't figure it out."

"I can shoot a gun?" He thinks it's cool. "I prefer a whip, like Indy."

"Stop it!" I say. "You're much more…"

"Much more what?"

I don't tell him the crazy killer he is going to become. I shouldn't have told him about the twelve men as well. What if he has a chance to become a different person?

"Oh." He jumps on his desk with his hookah hose in one hand. "I will kill them with this."

Some things never change. I am starting to worry Mrs. Tock is right. I will not be able to change anything.

"A brilliant idea." He examines his hookah. "I've always thought it could be a weapon. But I wouldn't tell anyone. They'd think I'm weird."

"How about love?" I ask him. "You remember loving Fabiola?"

"Who wants to love a nun in the Vatican?" he says. "Is that even legal?" Then his eyes glitter. "I'm really going to be that bad? Seducing a nun?"

"Forget about it." I rest my hands on my hips.

"What else do you know about me?"

This is when I nail it. "The Executioner." The most suppressed memories will always surface when tickled long enough.

The Pillar drops the hookah. His eyes are gleaming.

I take advantage of the moment and grip his hands. I pull off the gloves and point at his missing fingers. "Remember this?" It's odd that I don't even know what really happened to him. I was just told about the Pillar's missing fingers by Fabiola last week. She refused to tell me the whole story, though.

The Pillar shrugs. The shrug turns into inanimate features. Then into a darker part of him, not so much like in the future, but noticeable.

"I remember something," he says. "Can't fully remember it." He pulls off his glasses and throws them on the desk. "It hurts so much, though."

"I'm sorry to do this to you, but I need your help."

"I need to kill the Executioner, don't I?"

I nod.

"Why?"

"I'm not sure, but you may have been his child slave in some drug cartel in the past. Whether it was in Wonderland or the real world, I don't know."

"So Wonderland is real?" He sits back.

"It is."

"I can't believe it."

"Why? You seem to have persuaded half of the girls in Oxford it is."

"A hope. A child's wish. Reality is a bit scary. And I'm a Wonderlander?"

"Yes. The Pillar himself."

"That whack atop a mushroom."

"If you want to call yourself names, yes."

"Wait." He closes his eyes. "Why do I remember a book?"

"A book?"

"A book by Lewis Carroll." He stands up again and starts to rummage through his wall-long library, dropping books left and right. "If you're from the future you should know what I am searching for."

"I'm not sure. What book?"

"This!" He shows it to me. "Alice's Adventures Under Ground."

I am about to shriek. It's the same book he showed me in the future, the first time I met him.

"One of the few original copies in the world," the Pillar says. "Just remembered now when you told me. Why do I remember it now?"

I watch the dark smile on the Pillar's face. A nerdy professor about to turn into a madman and kill twelve people. He is staring at the same book that drove him mad. This time, I really need to sit down and contemplate. I realized I've just triggered the Pillar's madness.

Mrs. Tock is definitely right. The future can't be changed. It will always find a way.

# Chapter 69

*The Present: The Department of Insanity, Ha Ha Street, London*

Inspector Dormouse drank his fifth coffee in the last hour. Never had he felt the urge to stay awake like today. Since last week's incidents with the mad Carolus, he'd begun to realize that sleeping wasn't going to help him at his job. He needed to stay alert. Something was going on in this world. Something he needed to figure out.

He'd been tracing Alice and Pillar's past through the documents on his desk. Never mind they had fooled him into thinking she was a girl called Amy Watson and he was an animal rights activist called Petmaster. He'd figured out they were frauds last week. He'd also figured out they were mad and connected to some mysterious Wonderland War. Whatever that meant.

After dozing off again, Inspector Dormouse snapped awake and walked to the coffee machine, gulping himself another shot of caffeine. Staying awake was hard work, really. A pillow and a cushiony bed would be heaven right now.

But he had to get a grip of himself. He was about to discover something.

And there it was, right in front of him, in the Pillar's profile.

The controversial professor had killed twelve people. Why twelve? Who were they?

Inspector Dormouse sat sipping his coffee, flipping pages in the Pillar's profile. It mentioned the professor pleading insanity and ending up in Radcliffe Asylum. Inspector Dormouse wondered if that was what it was all about. The Pillar had killed those people to plead insanity in court and end up near this girl Alice for some reason.

But why kill? Weren't there easier ways to sneak into an asylum?

Flipping pages, he couldn't get the answer. Not right away. Not until he came about the victims' names and the locations of death. That was when the inspector had his suspicions. Could it be?

Inspector Dormouse tapped the file and said, "So that's why you killed them, professor." And before he could follow up with a conclusion, the inspector fell asleep again. Coffee definitely wasn't the answer for consciousness.

# Chapter 70

## *THE PAST: AN ALLEY IN OXFORD*

Despite the Pillar's dilemma with remembering the past, he does in fact know Jack's whereabouts. Turns out Jack is a well-known young hustler all over Oxford and London. Not in the ways I imagined, though. Jack is a card player of distinctive qualities.

I stand with the Pillar, peeking into an alley from the edges of a garbage can, watching Jack. He sits among a bunch of older men playing cards on the back of an abandoned vehicle.

"Five pounds for the next round." Jack bites on the tip of a matchstick, mocking the muscled man before him.

"Ten pounds," the man offers. "If I win this round of blackjack, I get ten pounds."

"And if I win?" Jack inquires.

"You get five."

"What kind of logic is that?"

"The logic of muscles." The man stretches out his broad torso. His gargoyle friends back him up with a laugh behind folded arms.

Jack is really thin. He looks mischievous and slick, but he wouldn't have a chance in a fight.

"I have a better idea," Jack says. "If I win, I take all of your clothes."

"What did you just say?" the man growled.

"In exchange, you get to beat the bonkers out of me if I lose." Jack winks. "I swear I won't file charges."

"Who bets this way?" The man frowns.

"A boy who's sure he is going to win."

"Are you even aware of what you will become if we beat you? You'd be lying flat on the floor."

"Just like this card on the table?" Jack lays down his first card.

"Rethink this, Jack," the man says. "You've got all those fluffy girls liking you back in school. They won't like you with a bruise for a nose and hole for an eye."

"Truth is, I need the money," Jack says. "And your heavy metal cha cha cha clothes look like they're worth a hundred pounds."

The semi-nerdy Pillar whispers in my ear, "This Jack is badass. Better than Indy."

I try not to roll my eyes. They hurt from doing this too much already. "Are we going to let him do this to himself?" I ask the Pillar. "Jack may need help."

"Help him if you want. I'm staying here," says a cowardly Pillar. "Besides, I think he is going to win."

But the Pillar is wrong. Whatever version of blackjack they're playing, Jack is losing fast. The muscular men roar with laughter and start knuckling their fingers.

"Here is your ten pounds." Jack grins.

"What?" the man says.

"You said you'd take ten if you won."

"No, that was the first deal. Then you said we could beat you if you lose."

"Who said that?" Jack says. "You guys must be dreaming."

"What? Are you calling us mad?"

"Think of it. Why would I play cards for you to beat me when you can just beat me whenever you want? You just misunderstood me."

The muscular men scratch their temples, thinking it over. "So we don't need to win to beat you?"

"Right on."

"Then no problem. Let's beat him up, boys."

"But hey." Jack raises his hands. "That's not a fair fight. And as strong and muscular as you are, you surely want a fair fight. You wouldn't brag about squashing a cockroach, right? It's just not good manners."

They scratch their heads again. "So what do you suggest we do?"

"I'll fight one man at a time."

"Deal." The man takes off his jacket, his muscles spilling over on the sides. "I'll go first."

"Hey," Jack says. "Come on. Look at you. You're twice my age, four times my size, six times my weight. In fact, you're the size of my whole family."

"So what now, Jack?"

"I can't fight you all at once. It's like you squishing a rat."

"Then how am I going to beat you, Jack?" The man starts to lose patience.

"I suggest I fight with just your arms first." He raps the man's arms. "Just about the right size. Your arms against the whole me."

"And where do you suggest the rest of me goes?"

"I don't know." Jack shakes his shoulders. "That's your problem. You could cut off your arm or something."

The man grunts, stepping forward.

"Okay, bad joke." Jack shrugs. "I have a better idea. Just hear me out."

"Last chance."

"You wouldn't be able to move your arm if it wasn't for your brain, right?"

"Come again?"

"The brain sends signals to an arm for it to move and punch someone. You know that, right?"

"Is that true?" the man asks his buddies.

They shake their shoulders. "How would we know?"

"It's true. Science, they call it," Jack explains.

"So what's the point?"

"The point is your arm wouldn't work without your brain. But your brain works without your arm."

"And?"

"Let's fight brain to brain."

"Why didn't you say so?" The man laughs. "You want us to fight like bulls. Come here, Jack. I'll crash your skull for giggles."

"Didn't quite mean that," Jack protests. "People usually use their brains, not fight with them."

"Now you're really losing me."

"I mean to play brain to brain. We need to simply go play cards again. See who wins, have this talk all over again, realize fights are useless, then play again."

The man's head whizzes around. "What?"

That's when Jack pulls out a set of cards and flicks them one after the other in their faces. It seems childish at first, until I realize the cards are covered with a thick substance that sticks to their faces. When they try to pull it off, it snaps at their skins.

The men begin to roar.

Jack runs out of the alley. It happens so fast I don't have a chance to call after him. When I'm about to, I see Jack jumping into the back of a car filled with girls.

And who do you think is driving it?

Lorina Wonder.

# Chapter 71

"You really like this boy," the Pillar comments behind me.

I watch Lorina's car drive away, and say nothing.

"Look," the Pillar says. "You came to me to ask me what to do with Jack. If you're really from the future, I suggest you let him go."

"You think so?"

"I do." He adjusts his glasses. "Better look for your Wonder, bring yourself home while I try to remember everything about myself."

I glance one last time at the empty street where Lorina's car once stood. Maybe he is right. "I think you're right, Pillar."

"See?" He is proud of himself.

"Logically, I should be the Bad Alice right now, looking for a bus full of students. But I'm not. I feel fine. Maybe I've been cured of my darkness."

"I'm not sure I'm following. But I'm with you all the way."

"Actually, it's you who I should thank." I pat him on the shoulder.

"Me?"

"You're the one who helped me become a better person in the future. You—"

"Stop!" the Pillar says. "Don't spoil the future for me. I already know I will kill twelve people."

"Maybe you know it for a reason. So you can prevent it."

"You think so?" He raises an eyebrow. But then his face dims. "No, I don't think so. I think I'm a badass, ruthless killer. I need to kill the Executioner."

"Shouldn't you remember why you want to kill him first?"

"I'm sure it'll all come to me." He taps the book in his hands. "So you want to eat ice cream?"

"Ice cream?" I try not to laugh. "You like ice cream?"

"Yes." He lowers his head and whispers, "It helps me with my hookah cravings. I think I'm addicted to smoke."

"Is that so?"

"Come on, Alice of Wonderland," he chirps. "Let me introduce you to the greatest invention of all time."

"Which is?"

"Licking ice cream. Not ice cream, but the act of licking it. Hazelnut and chocolate ice cream cones."

"I'll pass. I need to find my Wonder."

"Ah, that. What could it be? I *wonder*?"

I wheeze out half a laugh. "Even if I don't find it, I'm good. Maybe the Bad Alice isn't supposed to return to the present. I saved Jack. That's what matters."

"If you say so. It really confused me how you were going to kill him in the first place. Nothing in the events of this day suggests that."

"Actually, they do." My jaw tightens as I watch a black limousine pull over. I know who's inside it. I've seen it before, and I'm starting to experience a few wicked emotions in my chest.

The Pillar and I stare at the woman stepping out of the limousine while the street is suddenly swarming with Reds. It's the Queen of Hearts.

"Where do you think you're going?" she says.

"Who are you, woman?" the Pillar says.

The Queen slaps him with the back of her hand, and the poor professor lands next to the garbage can.

"What do you want?" I ask her.

"You know what I want," she says. "You'll not mess this up. You're going to be on that bus in less than an hour. Understand?"

"And if I don't understand?" I step up to her.

She smirks. "You know what the beauty of this moment is?"

"Enlighten me."

"That you're not much of the Bad Alice, so I don't fear you, but you're also not much of the Good Alice, so you won't mess up the plan."

"I'm not following."

"You've been injecting yourself with little doses of Lullaby so your family won't expose you as the Bad Alice," the Queen explains. "It was Mr. Jay's orders from the beginning. He thought you wouldn't overdo it. But your love for Jack made you want to resort to becoming good all the time. That's why you don't feel like getting on the bus. But now you will."

"Wait," I say. "Are you saying you know I'm from the future?"

"I do."

This part really dizzies me, because, according to the timeline, tomorrow I will stuff a bunch of Lullaby pills in her and she won't remember anything after. But today? "How could you possibly know?"

"Mrs. Tock told me." She smirks. "For the sake of accuracy, Mrs. Tock, the one you *met* tomorrow, found a way to tell herself today."

I have to blink at the confusion of the past-tense verb used with the word "tomorrow." But I get it. The future is resisting change. It's pushing me in every possible way to follow the timeline of killing the students.

Two Reds suddenly restrain me from behind and the Queen stuffs a mushroom in my mouth. They don't even need to force me to chew on it, as it melts instantly. Not just that. I find myself craving it, because it slowly turns me to my real self. The girl who works for Black Chess.

It's a terrible and conflicting feeling. The shift from here to there is like being high on drugs. I am not sure who I am now.

"It will take a while until you're fully yourself again," the Queen says. The Reds let go of me. "But we'll be watching you until you get on that bus."

I fall to my knees from the pain. The Pillar is lying comatose on the ground next to me.

"Why is it so important I kill my classmates on the bus?" I'm trying my best to use the better part in me, as long as it's possible.

"Don't ask, Alice," the Queen says. "No one questions their role in the Wonderland Wars. Not when working for Black Chess."

Resisting the need to vomit, I am aware I don't have much time before I fully turn into a Black Chess employee. The damned Mrs. Tock is right again. It seems like I'm destined to kill my classmates.

But at least I saved Jack.

The Queen returns to her car. I clench a fist and try to fight the pain in my stomach. Then the worst of my nightmares manifests itself.

"Alice?" Jack kneels down next to me. "What are you doing here?"

I raise my eyes and stare into his, seeing how concerned he is.

"Gosh, you look awful. What did you eat?"

My face reddens with pain. No words come out of me.

"Come on." He gently pulls me up. "We need to get you ready, or we'll miss the bus."

# Chapter 72

"It looks like things are going to work," Mr. Tick remarked, staring at Alice lying on the bed.

"The future always finds a way," Mrs. Tock added, secretly biting on one of his brownies behind his back.

"What are you two talking about?" Fabiola scowled.

"The Queen of Hearts corrected Alice's path, and now she is going to kill everyone on the bus," Mr. Tick said.

"Corrected the path? How?" Fabiola's mind was frying with all the paradoxes of time travel, which she wasn't interested in, not the slightest. All she cared about was Alice's death.

"It's a long and complicated story," Mr. Tick said. "All you need to know is that she met Jack and now they're going to get on the bus."

"And soon she'll kill them all," Mrs. Tock said around a mouthful.

"Are you eating my brownies?" Mr. Tick inquired.

"Ate your brownies, you mean." She giggled. "As for you, Fabiola, be very afraid. Once Alice kills her classmates, everything will go the way Black Chess planned it."

"How?" Fabiola said. "You still haven't got your keys."

"I'm sure the keys will show up along the way, now that she's returning to the Bad Alice again," Mrs. Tock said.

"Even so," Fabiola said. "The keys don't worry me. We'll fight over them in this life. As long as Alice doesn't find her Wonder, I'm not worried."

"I was just thinking about this, White Queen." Mr. Tick plunked two sugar cubes into his thirteenth cup of tea. "You may have not understood what her Wonder really is."

"What do you mean? Didn't you say her Wonder is the one thing she'll always be proud of in life?"

"Exactly." He turned the spoon, making clanging noises. "But that's the Wonder of a so-called good person."

"Explain yourself." Fabiola tensed.

"A good person's Wonder may simply be his children," Mrs. Tock said. "Or the one time they saved the life of a dog when it was in dire need."

"So?"

"So how about a bad person's Wonder?" Mr. Tick snickered like usual.

Fabiola grimaced. The implications were disastrous.

"Let me put it this way," Mr. Tick said. "The Bad Alice's Wonder may be different from the Good Alice's Wonder."

"Meaning, her Wonder at this time might be killing someone," Mrs. Tock explained.

"Like her classmates, for instance." Mr. Tick clanked his spoon against his china, as if he were calling boxers for the next round of the fight.

"Genius, Mr. Tick," Mrs. Tock said.

"I know, Mrs. Tock."

"Are you two saying that Alice's Wonder may be killing her classmates?" Fabiola said.

"It would be a Wonder in Black Chess's eyes," Mrs. Tock said.

"You've got to be shitting me."

"Love it when nuns swear." Mr. Tick smiled. "It means evil is winning."

"Me too, Mr. Tick. Would you please clank that spoon again? Sounds like Alice's time has come."

# Chapter 73

## *THE PAST: OXFORD STREETS*

"What do you mean you don't want to get on the bus?" Jack pulls me by my hand in the most enthusiastic way. "You've always wanted to take that ride. You said your life depended on it."

"Stop." I try to wriggle myself out of his embracing arms. "I thought you like Lorina?"

"Your sis?" Jack laughs. "I admit she keeps chasing me. But I only use her when I need her. Like a few minutes ago I was betting on cards with stupid men and lost the game. She was a good escape with your mummy's car."

So that was it?

"Look." He pulls out a handful of pounds. "I won that off the men."

"What's it for?"

"For us, Alice. Who else?" He keeps dragging me along the street.

"Us?"

"The trip, Alice. We're getting on that bus. I know you're worried about money, but once we're there, I'll take care of you."

"Jack." I finally stop. "Slow down, please."

Jack's face pales a little. "What is it? You changed your mind?"

"Changed my mind about what?"

"About us?"

Jack is only killing me — if I don't kill him in a few, that is.

"I thought you realized how much I love you," he says. "How can I explain this to you?"

"I — "

"I know. I know. I'm a crook. A thief. I don't even go to school. But I'll be a good man, Alice. You can't just let me go."

It's right now where I can stop it all. I just need to tell him I don't love him. I can tell him to freakin' walk away from me. Damn it. Why am I not saying it? It's just a few words. *I don't love you. I don't want to see you again.* Why can't I?

"Look." Jack pulls me closer. "Only you know me. Only you."

"And you don't know anything about me."

"I know enough. It's not like you can turn out to be worse than me."

"I *am* worse than you, Jack."

"Nice one." He flicks his nose against mine. "Now, don't be silly. The bus is coming."

And you're never getting out of it, Jack, if I'm on it.

"It's our time, Alice," Jack insists. "We need to have fun together. A life. We need to get on that bus. Hell, I don't know anyone who wouldn't want to get on it."

"I can't." The words slip out of me. "I just can't."

Jack gets the message this time. He realizes I'm not being bratty. He can read it in my eyes. "You're not in love with that old douche, are you?"

"Old douche?"

"That professor. What's his name?"

I stop myself from laughing. And though I can just tell him that I am, I can't bring myself to break his heart.

"So what's the problem, Alice?" Jack says.

Thinking of an answer, I suddenly notice we're near the bus station. It's a few feet away. That's it. And there, among the giggling girls waiting for the bus, the Reds stand everywhere, disguised as normal people. The Queen's limousine waits at the curb. And a woman in a Red fur stands on the opposite side. My instinct tells me Black Chess is all around, to make sure I will get on the bus.

"Alice, look at me. Tell me what's going on." Jack holds me tighter. "I'd die for you, Alice. Just tell me what's wrong."

*I'd die for you, Alice.* The words cling to my soul. My darker soul, which is suddenly surfacing.

*Why not?* I find myself thinking.

I've been manipulating this stupid boy for so long. Why not? Let him get on the bus. Let him die with the others.

Hail Black Chess.

Now I'm back. The real me. The one you should fear the most.

I pull Jack toward the bus station, imagining a scary rabbit staring back at me from a mirror. "Welcome back, Alice," the rabbit says.

# Chapter 74

Dr. Tom Truckle was enjoying his mock turtle soup when Fabiola crashed into his office. He wasn't sure who she was yet. He'd only seen her serving beer and cracking jokes in the Inklings a couple of times. He'd always joked she looked like a dark version of the famous Vatican nun. But, of course, she couldn't be her.

"I need your help." Fabiola stood by the door, her tattoos barely distracting from her impressively athletic body and good looks.

"Only my wife asks for help with a sword in her hand." He drooled some of the soup back into the bowl. "Want to be my next?"

"Shut up," Fabiola said. "Alice is about to find her Wonder."

"Alice?" He frowned. "Her what?"

"She has to die."

"Are we talking about the mad girl in the cell below?"

"You know she isn't in the cell below." Fabiola stepped up. "I know all about you. About the Pillar manipulating you into letting her out."

"Great." Tom dropped his spoon. "Excuse me if I need to pop another pill to talk to you."

"You're not going to do anything unless I tell you," Fabiola said.

"Trust me, the pill helps with all your Wonderland madness." He reached for the drawer but Fabiola stopped him, waving a threatening sword in the air.

"I know who you are, Tom," Fabiola said. "I know what Lewis told you about this asylum, so drop the mask."

Tom shrugged. Did others know about this? Lewis had never told him this Fabiola had anything to do with this. "What do you want?"

"Now we're talking." Fabiola leaned against the edge of his desk. "Like I said, Alice Wonder must die."

"Why?"

"You don't get to ask questions, Turtle," she mocked him. "You will only follow my orders."

"If you say so." He really needed that pill now.

"I will need an army to kill Alice when she wakes up."

"Wakes up?"

"I told you not to interrupt me."

Tom sat up, listening carefully.

"You did a good job, all those years, collecting sane people into the asylum," she said. "Now it's time to use them."

"Really?" Tom's eyes widened. So Lewis' prophecy was useful.

"Yes," she said. "I will need all the Mushroomers in your asylum."

"Need them?"

"Didn't you hear me?" Fabiola said. "Alice is coming back, and I'll need all your insane — or sane — patients to kill her."

# Chapter 75

## *THE PAST: OXFORD STREETS*

It's hard to explain this feeling inside me. It's harder to explain how good I feel, dragging Jack toward the bus station. Old and scattered memories of the Bad Alice flood my soul as I am about to kill my classmates.

As we head to the station, a thinner, weaker Good Alice tries to oppose me, trying to understand why I am supposed to kill those on the bus. But things happen so fast, I can't locate such an old memory I've devoted my life to — my darker life, that is.

"I'm glad you changed your mind." Jack holds my hand, now standing among others at the station.

"Me too." I peck him on the cheek, my evil eyes sparkling with all the wrong emotions. It's weird how darkness feels so powerful. It reminds me of Fabiola warning me of getting stained when looking darkness in the eyes. The poor woman discreetly hoped I wasn't the Real Alice all this time. What an old, mentally conflicted nun.

The bus is supposed to arrive in ten minutes. The innocent passengers have no idea of their morbid fates. Most of the passengers are girls. In fact, there are only three boys about to get on the bus. I wonder why.

Please don't do this, Alice. You're not her anymore.

That weak and stupid voice of the Good Alice inside me—it annoys me. If I only had the means to choke her. But that would be choking myself, too. And hell, I freakin' like me. I like the Bad Alice. Once I kill for Black Chess, I should take some time to immerse myself in the bloody memories of the past.

A couple of memories loom before me. Me, back then in Wonderland, after the events of the circus, mercilessly slaying a few humans. Why would I give up on such power? And I thought I was an insane girl buried underground, thinking she could save lives.

"Alice." Jack squeezes my hand.

"Yes, baby?"

"Do you want your necklace back?"

"Necklace?"

"The one you gave me last week," Jack says. "You said it's important."

"Of course I want it back." I don't have the slightest idea what he is talking about.

But Jack doesn't get a chance to give it back. Suddenly he falls to his knees, clutching at his stomach.

"What's wrong, Jack?" I say, but it's not like I care. I am just annoyed at the plan going wrong.

"My stomach hurts so much."

"All of a sudden?" I say. "Man up, Jack. The bus is coming soon."

"It hurts." He moans. "I think I need to visit the bathroom."

"You what?"

Jack hurtles through the crowd in a flash. He needs to use the loo that bad. It happens so fast that I'm perplexed. My plan can't go wrong. I don't know, but Jack has to die along with the passengers, even though I know he isn't the target. I just don't want to change the course of events. I must have had a reason to kill him in the past, and the reason should remain now.

"He's gone to the bathroom?" A panting Pillar shows up, adjusting his glasses again.

"Can you believe this?" I say.

"I can." The Pillar grins. "It was me."

"You?"

"I slipped something into his drink," he says. "A Chinese herb I use when constipated. He isn't coming out of there anytime soon."

"What? Why?"

"Didn't you want him off the bus?" The Pillar drools like a bulldog.

I slap him on the face and then kick him out on the street. "Can you get any dumber?"

Suddenly his girl fans are upset with me, pushing me sideways, and kneeling down to help their Wonderland believers.

"Duh!" I shout.

I could easily kill them here right now. But they have to die on the bus for some reason. I have to get Jack back. And fast. The bus is coming.

# Chapter 76

*THE PRESENT: RADCLIFFE ASYLUM*

Tom stood watching Fabiola lecture the Mushroomers. She was telling them of the Bad Alice and all the details they hadn't known about earlier. The Mushroomers, holding to the bars, listened tentatively.

"So we're not mad?" one of them asked.

"Not the least," Fabiola said. "It was this man who framed you and brought you here." She pointed at Tom.

The Mushroomers produced noises of anger and were about to shoot laser beams out of their eyes at him, Tom thought. "I was asked to do this," he explained. "Lewis Carroll told me."

It didn't seem to change anything. If they were set free now, they were going to eat him alive.

"Tom is right," Fabiola broke in. "He was instructed by Lewis Carroll to make an army out of you. You do know who Lewis is, right?"

"The madman!" all the Mushroomers said in one breath.

It was then when Tom realized the Mushroomers had lost it. He wasn't that surprised, though. Locking a sane man in a room for too long and expecting him to come out as sane as he was before was a big joke. The shock therapy, the lonely nights, and all the things they went through. Who wouldn't lose their mind?

"What's going on, Tom?" Fabiola said.

"I think we're too late," he said. "I don't think they will be useful."

"Another dead end." Fabiola puffed.

"It's the truth," Tom said. "First of all, I don't think they will kill Alice if you let them out. I think they like her a lot. They will kill us instead."

"Are you saying Lewis' plan didn't work?"

"He was a good man, but we have to admit he was as bonkers as the rest of us."

"Then you're as bonkers for following his instructions."

"A friend of mind once said, 'We're all mad here.'"

"Shut up, Turtle!" Fabiola was losing it. Tom thought she'd better go back to being a nun. It helped her calm down. "What am I going to do now? Who is going to kill Alice if she comes back?"

"My question is why don't you do it yourself?" Tom proposed. "I see you're ready to kill for your cause."

The impact of Tom's words twitched every pore of Fabiola's face. He thought he even saw her hand tremble. The White Queen seemed to have developed a certain affection for Alice. That's what this really was about. Fabiola's weakness was now her affection for a Bad Alice.

*Damn that Pillar*, Tom thought. *The man is a genius.* Why not, when Tom couldn't yet figure out how the Pillar entered and left his cell with no one ever knowing how?

Fabiola dropped her sword. "I hate you," she said.

"Come again?" Tom said.

"I hate you for making me love someone so bad."

"I'm not sure what you mean," Tom said. "Are you sure you're talking to me?"

"Of course I'm not talking to you. I'm talking to the Pillar, wherever he is."

# Chapter 77

## *THE PAST: BUS STATION, OXFORD*

Jack surprises me, returning within seconds. He is still holding his stomach but stands next to me in the station. "I think I can take the pain," he says. "I know how much the trip means to you."

I don't give a damn. It's good that he is back. I grip his hand tighter so I don't lose him this time. I don't even thank him.

"What happened to your professor?" He points at the girls gathering around the Pillar, making sure he is all right.

"Don't bother," I tell Jack, then I turn to the girls. "Hey, you don't want to miss the bus. Come over here."

One of them swears at me, describing how cruel I am. As if I care. The rest of the girls are too naive to comment or get back at me. Frankly, all I see is jealousy. They're jealous of Jack's devotion to me. How I managed to make him love me, I can't remember.

Across the street, the Queen's limousine still waits. The Reds are in every corner, watching me. Even Lorina and Edith are standing by the curb. Why hasn't the bus arrived yet?

Don't do it, Alice. The nagging voice arises again. You can change the future for the better. You can still purge your sins.

I want to kill that stupid girl inside me, but don't have an idea how. But it doesn't matter; soon enough the bus will arrive and we'll get this over with. I'm in control. The Bad Alice is in control.

No you aren't, the nagging voice says. You really aren't.

The nagging voice is too confident this time. I wonder why. It scares me. Why is my good side so confident I will fail?

Look at him, it says. Just look at him.

Look at whom? I tilt my head and stare at Jack. He is still aching, but he's nothing but a ring on my finger now. I'll tell him where to go and what to do. Not him, the voice says. But him.

Who? I look left and right, panicking. Is the Good Alice trying to play games with my mind?

There is no one here that can change my mind. No one.

I keep repeating this to myself... until I see *him.*

Not Jack, but the boy the Good Alice is pointing at. A boy who is going to change my life. How? I'm not sure.

I find myself staring at a boy wearing an exquisite black hat. He is standing across the street. He has a confident and rough attitude about him, but that's not what attracts me. I know him.

I know him in the strangest ways.

It's not even logical that I recognize him. But I do. I can't forget the voice of the man I'm going to marry in the future. *Did you wake up, baby?* I remember him saying when I was in the future in the Wonderland Compound.

I'm staring at the boy I don't know but will change my life.

But even so, the Bad Alice in me is still stubborn enough to complete her mission. I am still determined to kill everyone on the bus. Who said I have to marry this boy in the future? Who said he has an influence on me?

You really don't get it. The nagging voice is laughing at me now. Wait until he crosses over to the bus station. You're toast. The Good Alice will win. It's going to be painful, but I will win.

The boy does cross the street. And with every closer look at him, I begin to understand how the Good Alice will win.

Again, in the strangest ways.

With each step closer, I see the boy in a very different way. I recognize him and relate to him — although I've never seen him before — in the most emotional ways.

It's in his eyes. It's in his cheeks. In his walk. It's in my children I see through him.

I gasp, noticing Lily has his eyes. Tiger has his pompous and manly walk. Lily has his cheekbones. Tiger has his pursed-lipped smile. I can go on forever.

# Chapter 78

Unconsciously, I let go of Jack's hands. It's illogical. Unexplainable. As mad as love is. The Good Alice surfaces.

Whether I'm going to marry this boy or really have his children in the future, only one thing matters now. I'm myself again. The self I choose to be, not what Black Chess wants me to be. Jack has to live. So do the girls on the bus.

"Something wrong, Alice?" Jack asks me.

I fill my eyes with his gorgeous face. I want to tell him that he is going to live. I want to tell him that I'm okay. Everything is going to be all right.

But he wouldn't understand. His love for me is too strong.

Not only do I know that from my feelings, or the way he came back from dead for me, but from what happens to the Cheshire in the future. Jack's love for me is so strong it will soften the cat's heart.

Which means Jack will never let go of me in the future.

"Why are you looking at me like that?" Jack's eyes sparkle.

I know why. Because I know Jack will never stop loving me. And even if I stop him from getting on the bus today, even if I don't kill him, he will never be safe around me. Who guarantees I don't turn into the Bad Alice five minutes from now? And if not, Jack could be easily hurt in the future, whether by the Cheshire or anyone else.

I know why I'm staring this way at him. Because it's the last time I will be staring at him so lovingly. The last time he will love me at all.

Slowly I turn away from Jack, unable to imagine how he is going to feel a minute from now. True, I won't kill him. But I will do worse. I will make him not love me again.

Stepping ahead, I wave at my future husband, the pompous boy, and wrap my arms around him.

The boy welcomes me. Either because he is used to girls doing this to him, or because it's just fate we can't change. I pull his head closer to me and kiss him. The boy kisses me back, and I start to make out with him in the craziest ways.

I am so blunt about it, it looks like I do this a lot. Hisses saturate the air around us. Girls gasp, others whisper, and Jack... I have no idea what's happening to him.

A tear threatens to squeeze out of my eye. But I lock it in. Jack has to believe I mean this. And the boy, well, he is enjoying this a lot.

Images of Tiger and Lily flash before my eyes. Maybe I am not going to marry the one I love, but the one whose children I will love.

After the kiss, and the incredible scene I made, I slowly catch Jack's reaction from the corner of my eye.

Oh, Jack. I'm so sorry.

Jack is simply dying in front of my eyes. The damage is done. Mission accomplished. Everyone lives happily ever after, except Jack.

# Chapter 79

"She sacrificed her love to save the students on the bus," said the mousy chauffeur, having just arrived from eavesdropping on Mr. Tick and Mrs. Tock in the Inklings.

The Pillar, sitting in the back, smiled. He had both hands rested on his cane. His smile was thin, the chauffeur thought. But he understood. The situation was complicated. Alice, evil or good, was doomed.

"So is that it?" The chauffeur felt uncomfortable about the Pillar's silence. "She saves the world, fails to find her Wonder, and ends up dead in the past?"

The Pillar tapped his cane. Said nothing.

"That's not fair," the chauffeur said. "I mean, she really changed the world. Why does she have to die, let alone live in this kind of misery?"

The Pillar resorted to silence again and again.

"Shouldn't we see changes in this future because of the things she changed?" the chauffeur tried one last time.

The Pillar leaned back, staring out of the window. It had started to rain, and looking outside was like looking at a mirror buried in the mist. "You ever been in love?" the Pillar said.

The chauffeur shrugged. "Once."

"Really?"

"Of course. Everyone must have been in love once."

"Not an ugly mouse like you."

The chauffeur knew the Pillar was joking. "I fell in love with a girl, mousy like me. We suited each other. In fact, she loved me a lot."

"If so, why aren't you with her now?"

"Because I'm with you, professor."

"Why are you with me?"

"I believe in your cause—morally controversial, yes, but I'd like to help."

"I didn't know you were a miserable liar," the Pillar said.

"Liar?"

"You're not here because of me. You're here because of the money I pay."

"What's wrong with a man needing a job?"

"I'll tell you what's wrong," the Pillar said. He leaned forward, one hand gripping the back of the passenger seat. "You're not spending time with the one you love, thinking that making money and securing your future will help you prosper, so you can finally spend time with her."

"Professor." The chauffeur shrugged. "What are you telling me?"

"Go back home," the Pillar said. "Give me the keys, and go back to your loved one. Forget about me and Alice. This war that's coming isn't for everyone, unless you're really ready."

"Ready for what?"

"To give up on your loved ones."

# Chapter 80

## THE PAST: BUS STATION, OXFORD

Making out so bluntly with my future husband is like reaching the last rung on the ladder of insanity — let alone the fact I just said *future husband*.

My lips on that boy are in severe pain. A strange pain. I close my eyes, wishing Jack would just disappear behind me. Hoping he gets the message and hates me for the rest of his life.

But Jack doesn't.

He taps me on the shoulder. I try not to turn around. I'd prefer he walks away with my back to him.

"Hey," the boy says. "She's mine."

I come to understand the boy and Jack might get into a fight. So I give in and turn to face Jack.

Keep the tears locked inside, Alice. Just for a minute. If Jack sees you crying he'll figure out something is wrong.

"Is that why you were surprised I came back from the bathroom?" Jack's pain is painted like a Picasso on his face. "Is that why you suddenly didn't want to get on the bus?"

"I—"

I have nothing to say.

Lorina takes the opportunity and backs Jack up. I can't quite hear what she says. All my senses are focused on Jack's pain. Generally, she is calling me all kinds of bad things.

Jack's eyes lock with mine. He must be seeing a stupid teenage girl, reckless and selfish. I see beautiful eyes that will enjoy a prosperous life and will not die young.

The tension breaks with the bus's ticket thrown at my face. It's not Lorina who does it. But Jack. Lorina smiles broadly and takes Jack's arm.

"I never want to see you again," Jack says. "I should have known. You're weird."

"She is mentally cuckoo," Lorina offers. Her friends laugh. "Trust me, I know. She's my sister."

"I should've listened to the rumors," Jack says.

"Rumors?" It's all I can say.

"They said you were some kind of a witch or something. You and your Wonderland creeps."

"Let's go, Jack," Lorina says. "You don't need this trip. I have a surprise for you."

Jack's last stare at me is full of disappointment. Borderline hatred. I'm sure it can't be fixed in the future now.

Go away, Jack. Go with Lorina. Stay alive.

My future husband senses the tension and holds me before I collapse under the weight of my pain. I pretend I like it, watching Jack walk away.

With every step, I get this warm feeling up my nostrils. I realize it's blood. My time in the past is scant. I may have saved Jack, and the bus, but I haven't found my Wonder. I haven't saved myself.

But Jack returns for one last scene. An unexpected one, really. "Here." He hands me a necklace. "It's yours, and I don't want anything that reminds me of you."

"Mine?" I stare at it, remembering he talked to me about it earlier. But I don't recognize it.

"You don't even remember you gave it to me?" Jack says. "I bet you give it to all the boys."

"What's this for?" I stare at the necklace in my hand and realize there is a key attached to it. The key has a drawing of the Six Keys on it. On the back is that strange number 14 again. This is the key to where I keep the rest of Six Impossible Keys.

The irony.

I stand with the necklace in my hand. The keys. The reason why I embarked on this journey from the beginning. I've exchanged Jack's life for the keys. No wonder they never found the rest of them. I kept them with Jack.

"I don't want the necklace," I scream at Jack. The pain is too strong. I don't know why I do it, but I throw the keys back in his face. They'll end up in Black Chess's hands if I keep them with me. Jack catches them, as if a tiny piece of him still wants to carry a memory of me.

Then he disappears.

My bleeding intensifies and I begin to feel dizzy. In only minutes I'll die, it seems. All I need now is to make sure the bus is safe.

I watch it arrive. The yellow school bus slows down by the curb. Most girls forget about the drama, excited by the trip they're about to take.

You did it, Alice. You did it.

I watch the girls get on the bus, my nose bleeding faster, but my heart is fluttering with victory. It's hard to imagine that I started this journey looking for a bunch of keys. Here I am, ending up with a bitter victory. But it's the right thing to do.

Without me on the bus, the future can change. Who said we can't change the past, Mrs. Tock?

# Chapter 81

THE PRESENT: INSIDE THE INKLINGS, OXFORD

"Did we just get the keys back?" Mr. Tick squinted at the dying Alice on the table.

"I'm not sure, Mr. Tick," his wife said. "Alice found the keys, but I think she threw them back to Jack."

"She also looks like she is going to pass on killing her classmates." Mr. Tick didn't look happy about it.

"Can't have all the cake, Mr. Tick."

"Of course I can have all the cake." He pointed at the brownie in his hand. "I always do. Figure out a way for Alice to kill her classmates and make sure she gets the keys."

"I don't know how to do that, Mr. Tick."

"Mr. Jay will be very upset."

"Margaret hired us to send Alice back in time to get the keys. She never said anything about keeping the timeline intact."

"But this will change a lot of things."

"I know, Mr. Tick. She will also die without killing her classmates. Because she will not have found her Wonder."

"Which means we will not even get the keys, if she has them."

"We don't need to, Mr. Tick. We know that the keys are with Jack."

"So?"

"Last I heard, the Cheshire managed to possess Jack's body. With a few tweaks and digging into his mind, the Cheshire will know where they are."

"That's genius, Mrs. Tock. But how about Alice? Doesn't Black Chess want their fiercest warrior back?"

"Can't help her now," Mrs. Tock said. "Like I said, if she doesn't kill her classmates, she dies."

"She is already dying." He pointed at Alice on the bed. "Look at how fast she is bleeding."

"Farewell, Bad Alice," Mrs. Tock said. "We'll miss you. You were real fun."

"Look at the endless number of kids she inspired for a century and a half," Mr. Tick said. "Did the kids know she was the Bad Alice?"

"Some did."

Mr. Tick let out a long sigh, took another brownie bite, then combed his hairies. "I guess that's it, then. Alice dies and we get the keys from Jack."

"I believe so, too."

"I'm just really unhappy with the passengers on the bus staying alive," he said. "I don't think I've seen someone capable of changing the past so dramatically. It's always been a few small changes, but not enough to change the course of the future."

"I agree, Mr. Tick. We all know those on the bus must die." Then an idea hit her. She rested a forefinger on her lips as if she'd discovered time itself. "Don't you think time won't let her change the past?"

"What do you mean?"

"I mean that the future always finds a way to stay on course. Rule number 47 in the *Wonderlastic Guide to Time Travels*."

"I read the rule, Mrs. Tock. But every rule has an exception."

"Maybe." She shrugged. "Maybe not."

# Chapter 82

Instead of slowly withering away, the terrible Alice inside me surfaces again. I guess it's because of my weakness that I can't oppose her now.

With blood trickling down my cheeks, I stand up and push my future husband away, about to catch up to the bus I am supposed to kill everyone on.

Talk about schizophrenic.

The boy holds me back for some reason. "You're still bleeding," he says. "You need a doctor."

I push him off me, realizing I still have enough strength to get the mission done. He falls back. "I really have no idea why I will marry you in the future," I say, standing up.

"Wow, hold your horses, girl," the boy says. "Not so fast. We were just fooling around."

I don't pay attention to him and run after the bus. All around me, Black Chess are still watching me, waiting for me to make it happen. Although I'm in evil mode, I wonder again and again why I have to kill those on the bus.

I run after the bus, realizing that I'm limping. Why not? I'm dying. Slower, I limp like a mad girl with blood on her face.

People make way for me. They don't want to have anything to do with me.

The last girl gets on the bus as I cling to the rail on the back. I'm going to get on it. It's the only meaning in the Bad Alice's life. It's the only way that I can live and return to the present, I suddenly realize. If I have no Wonder as a Good Alice then I bet it's the Bad Alice with the Wonder of killing her classmates.

The bus starts up and I cling harder to the rail, my legs scraping against the asphalt.

My knees hurt like hell. I should be dead already. I am trying to gather the strength to climb up. The girls in the back window stare at me as if I am terrorist. Well, I am. A Wonderland Monster.

I manage to pull myself up, bending my knees, and begin to climb up toward the top of the bus, like a poisonous spider who's come to finish the job.

"Let me in!" I pound on the glass. I must look like a demon now. "Let me in!"

The bus is full of girls. Why girls? Why do they have to die? Who are they?

One of the girls is so scared she submits to my threats and actually tries to open the back window. I smile wickedly at her, encourage her to speed it up.

Here she goes. Just a little wider, and I can set my foot inside.

But I don't.

Someone pulls me by my legs. I slip back, dropping on that someone behind me in the middle of the street, watching the bus fly away.

"No!" I scream, reaching out.

"It's all right." The Pillar holds me tight, both of us lying on our backs. "Let it go, Alice. Just let it go."

When he calls my name, I don't know which Alice he is talking to. It's worse than not knowing whether I'm mad or not.

The Pillar's grip is strong. He is more embracing me than keeping me away.

"The bus is gone," the nerdy Pillar says. "Whatever the reason you feel you need to catch it, there'll always be another."

"No, there isn't," I say, knowing it's too late. I possess no more strength to go after it. I don't really know what I'm doing anymore. I don't know who I am or what I want.

"The girls on the bus will live," I mumble.

"They will," the Pillar says. "Now just calm down. It will all be okay."

*And it should,* the Good Alice reminds me. Like the Pillar said, I just need to let go. I did all I could, saved a boy, a bus, and resisted a great evil inside me—although I am not sure which part of me surfaces most of the time.

But it's all right. The bus is about to disappear over the horizon.

It's okay. No harm will be done.

"I think I changed so many things in the future," I tell the Pillar, standing up.

"You think so?" He tilts his head. "I once read the future can never be changed."

And he is right, because far in the distance, looking over his shoulder, I see the bus veering off the road and crashed into a building.

# Chapter 83

"What happened?" Fabiola said.

Now that she had no means of using the Muhsroomers to kill Alice, she had come back, wanting to make sure the evil girl wouldn't return.

"The strangest thing." Even Mrs. Tock was surprised by the incident in the past.

"What do you mean? Speak up."

"I think..." Mr. Tick squinted. "I think Alice didn't kill her classmates on the bus."

"That's great news," Fabiola said. "It means she hasn't found her Wonder. It means she will not wake up again."

"It's not quite that simple," Mr. Tick said. "I also think that everyone on the bus died anyway."

"What are you talking about?"

"You see," Mrs. Tock began, "Alice didn't get on the bus, so she didn't kill her classmates, but even so, the bus crashed and exploded."

"That's impossible. It doesn't make any sense." Fabiola gripped her sword tighter, staring at the dying Alice on the bed. This was so hard for her. Her past, and the secrets she knew, obliged her to kill Alice now. But she just couldn't.

"Sense has nothing to do with time," Mr. Tick explained. "Time does what it likes."

"When it likes," Mrs. Tock added.

"Not a tick too soon."

"Not a tock too late."

"I need real answers," Fabiola said. "Something that I understand. If Alice wasn't on the bus, why did it veer off the road?"

"Why?" Mrs. Tock shook her shoulders. "I have no answer to that."

"But we know who did this," Mr. Tick said.

"Who, then?" Fabiola had to know.

"You won't believe it," Mr. Tick said.

"Carolus Loduvicus, although he jumped off the bus and didn't die himself," Mrs. Tock said. "He had always been the other Wonderlander on the bus with Alice."

"And I've always wondered why Carolus got on that bus, Mrs. Tock," Mr. Tick said.

"Me too. His presence on the bus is a mystery."

"But it does have a meaning," Mr. Tick said.

"It does?"

"Time is so slick it put Carolus on the bus so that if any of us, time travelers, ever wanted to change the past, it would always have a backup plan. Carolus. Time is so devious, Mrs. Tock."

"That's why we love working for it." Mrs. Tock snickered. "Time is never on your side. It's only on its own side. The future always finds a way to stay the same."

"I don't care about any of this," Fabiola said. "I need you to answer me this: did Alice find her Wonder?"

"Of course not," Mr. Tick said. "Her classmates died, but she didn't do it. Alice is pretty much dead. Evil or good. No Wonder. I'd be writing her obituary if I were you."

Hearing this, Fabiola collapsed on the chair. She finally had the results she'd sought. But she didn't know whether to love or hate the situation. She ran her hands over Alice's wide-open eyes and brushed them to a close. "Good night, Alice Wonder. I'll always hate myself for wanting you dead, but it's the right thing to do."

# Chapter 84

"What do you mean she died?" Margaret yelled at Carolus on the phone.

Carolus explained what Mr. Tick and Mrs. Tock had told him. He didn't tell her it was him who'd crashed the bus, though — and lived. He didn't see the point, and he didn't even remember doing it.

Margaret took a moment to assess the situation. She hardly cared about Black Chess or Alice. She cared to have good enough results so she could get back what was hers from the Queen. "And the key?" she asked.

"The keys are with Jack. We don't know what he's done with them. But the Cheshire will fix that."

"So my plan worked."

"I'd say it did. You promised the keys to the Queen. And now we know where they are."

Margaret let out a long sigh. "Okay, Carolus. Take a break now. I have an important meeting with the Queen."

# Chapter 85

The Queen cried herself to death in her room. Her tears were piercing bubbles, splashing against every wall in her chamber. Her dogs eagerly waited for the salty tears to slide down the walls, so they could lick them. They hadn't eaten or drunk anything for a while.

"Such a loss," the Queen told herself, dialing Mr. Jay's number. "I wonder how he will take the news."

"Yes?" Mr. Jay answered.

The Queen told him about Alice's death. The man's silence extended for a few uncomfortable breaths on the line. "Is that confirmed?"

"She is dead. I'm sorry," the Queen said. "I wished she wasn't."

"A shameful loss for Black Chess."

"I know. Winning the war will be much harder now."

"Alice has always been my favorite. The things she has done for us after the circus. I will always remember her. I wish there was someone to blame for her death."

"The Pillar," the Queen said. "He's the one who turned her mind, almost converted her to one of the Inklings."

"That's not quite true," Mr. Jay said. "Alice had once been an Inkling before she joined Black Chess. She didn't become one of us until the incident after the circus. You could say she had good and evil in her all the time."

The Queen nodded silently.

"Also, we may have never found her if it weren't for the Pillar," Mr. Jay said. "None of us was sure it was her."

"That damn Lullaby pill, and Lewis' curse to make us forget. I wonder how the Pillar knew she was the Real Alice."

"Maybe he didn't. It could be a stroke of luck."

"I doubt that. So are we going to do something about him now?"

"Something like what?"

"If you allow me to chop off his head, it'd be most Jub Jub."

"No." Mr. Jay's voice was firm. "Don't ever underestimate the Pillar. He didn't get into this to only convert Alice. The war is just starting. He is full of secrets. So tell me, do we have the keys?"

"The Cheshire is working on it. He says Jack's mind is a bit tricky."

"Don't trust the Cheshire either."

"I understand. I have my eyes on him." The Queen hesitated. "However, I have a request."

"Listening."

"I want to organize a respectable funeral for Alice."

"I understand, but it would expose us to the Inklings' forces. Who knows if they have other plans for us?"

"No one will notice. Kids and families will think it's a memorial for Alice in Wonderland from the book. To us, Black Chess, we'll be honoring our Real Alice."

"I don't mind. When are you planning on it?"

"Right away. It's going to be an exceptional Alice Day in the whole world next week."

# Chapter 86

The Cheshire sat alone on a bank. His head was still spinning from all the emotions and love in Jack's head. He'd heard about Alice's death and her sacrifice to make Jack hate her. But he hadn't witnessed any changes yet.

Mr. Tick and Mrs. Tock had told him changes in the future took some time. They didn't happen right away like in movies. Now the Cheshire cherished every last moment of Jack still loving Alice, knowing that soon this love would turn to hate.

He closed his eyes, still searching the corridors of Jack's mind. Searching for whatever made him come back from the dead.

And here it was. The Cheshire listened to Jack's mind.

I forgive you for killing me, Jack's voice said. But was that all? I came to tell you where I kept the keys.

The Cheshire's mind brightened with knowledge. He listened to the whereabouts of the keys and what they were for. The Cheshire was in awe. He couldn't believe it.

His eyes flew open. Would he tell Black Chess or the Inklings about it? Or would he take the power for himself?

Slowly, the Cheshire's body was hurting. He knew what was going on. The changes Alice had made in the past were starting to manifest in this world. And since Jack never died in this new version of life, he never came back for Alice, and the Cheshire never possessed him.

Mind bending stuff, even for the sneaky cat.

The Cheshire fell to his knees, knowing he had to posses another soul as soon as possible. Or he would simply die.

Clasping his face, the Cheshire realized he'd been tricked by the greatest murderer of all. He'd been tricked by time. Never a tick too soon. Never a tock too late.

# Chapter 87

Mrs. Tock and Mr. Tick watched the Cheshire fall to his knees, wondering if they should help him.

"It's a shame that the evil cat was that much of a fool," Mr. Tick said.

"Time befriends no one," Mrs. Tock said. "But I really had so much fun today, Mr. Tick. It was a timely adventure."

"Me too, Mrs. Tock." He held her hand. "We should do this again some time."

"Really?" Mrs. Tock's eyes brightened. "When?"

"A couple of hundred years from now," he said.

"Why not? We have all the time in the world."

"Which is pretty boring," he said. "But not as long as we're together. Ticking and tocking all the time."

Mrs. Tock laid her head on his chest and sighed. "Since you've finally admitted I make your life better, I have a confession, Mr. Tick."

"After all this *time*?" he mocked her lovingly.

"I know why you can't grow hair anymore."

Mr. Tick grimaced. "You know?"

"I have to confess it's because of me. I didn't want you flirting with younger girls. So I —"

"So you did what?"

"It's the tea you drink all night and day. It has a substance that causes baldness."

Mr. Tick was shocked. Even upset. He pulled his arm away and paced away from her.

"Mr. Tick!" she called after him. "I can make it grow back. Black pepper and olive oil will fix it!"

She ran after him. The Cheshire was still choking to death behind her.

# Chapter 88

The Queen had just finished her speech about Alice. The crowd and kids clapped, thinking she was talking about the stubborn seven-year-old Alice in the books. Every news reporter in the world wondered why the Queen wept.

"I will always miss Alice," the Queen said, flashing cameras surrounding her. "She will be always a part of my past, present, and future."

"Do you plan to build a statue of her?" a reporter asked.

The Queen thought it over for a moment. It seemed like a good idea, but hell no. She wouldn't make the people of England think there was someone as important as her in this life. She suddenly realized she didn't care about Alice. What was she doing?

Her face twitched and she yelled out, "Off with their heads."

The kids began to laugh. "Why is the Queen of England acting as if she were the Queen of Hearts?"

"She is mad," a child began to cheer. His friends liked the idea. Why couldn't be they were all mad in this world? They began singing. "We're all mad here.

\*\*\*

Fabiola stood next to the March Hare. He had woken up after Mr Tick and Mrs Tock got what they wanted.

"I can't believe she is the Real Bad Alice," the March Hare said. "I thought she was a sweet girl who believed she was Alice. I liked the idea a lot."

"You're naïve, Jittery. That's all. I will need you to grow up into a man." Fabiola said. "Now that Alice is dead, the Wonderland Wars have just begun. Us against Black Chess."

The March's ears stood erect again. Fighting Black Chess without Alice scared him. "I wonder who this Mr. Jay really is."

"I think I have an idea," Fabiola said. "I won't sleep well until I know who he is. So far he is the man behind Black Chess. We need to find him, or we will never win the war."

"Things got a lot complicated," The March said. "What are we going to do, White Queen? We're almost powerless."

"It's a shame you'd say that knowing who I am."

The March Hare shrugged. Of course he knew. The past was shadowing the future again. Clashes were unavoidable. Masks had been taken off, and there was no going back. "I know." He nodded, about to cry. "I just can't believe this sweet girl was Alice."

# Chapter 89

## *THE PRESENT: TOM TOWER, OXFORD*

I'm up in Tom Tower, watching the world below. This is the place where the Pillar once stood, shouting and warning the world of an upcoming war, yet no one paid attention. Things have changed. The world is talking about the possibility of a Wonderland War now. If they only knew what's coming.

But I'm not here to watch the world. I am standing here to watch Jack on the other side of the street. This is the present time. The now we should cherish. But it hurts so much. Jack is on the other side of the street, playing cards and hustling other people. I would love to run to him and throw myself in his arms. But I'd be ruining all that I worked for in the past.

I tell myself that I should be happy for him. He is alive and well. He isn't a ghost of a boy who died in a bus accident anymore. Eventually I will let him go. I know that.

I am also grateful I'm alive. Even though I didn't find my Wonder, somehow time let me live and return to the present moment.

I remember waking up in the Inklings room, all alone after Mr. Tick and Mrs. Tock had left. Even Fabiola had gone to do something. They thought I was already dead and were preparing to bury me. I woke up and left immediately.

In all cases, I'm everyone's enemy now.

Black Chess will hunt me if they know I am back as the Good Alice. The Inklings will hunt me thinking I am the Bad Alive, and that I can never change.

Back to square one, I tell myself. Back to where I am the loneliest hero in the world.

How I survived without finding my Wonder, I still don't know.

Silently, the Pillar arrives and stands next to me. We share the view of the world in silence. It's still good to have someone whom I can enjoy the silence with.

"You're a tock too late," I say.

"Or a tick too soon," he says.

"So you read the *Alice Under Ground* book, went mad, and still killed people," I say. "Some things never change."

"True," the Pillar says. "Believe it or not, the things you changed are very little. In this new version of the future, everything is still almost the same."

"That's what Mrs Tock said."

"In this version you and I still met in an asylum. I killed twelve people and entered as a patient. I asked Truckle for you and persuaded you that you were a hero. We saved so many lives, like in the earlier timeline."

"How so? If the bus exploded without me, I couldn't have ended up in the asylum again."

"But you did. The people waiting at the station told the authorities about the mad girl running hysterically after the bus. The court suspected you were an accessory to whoever exploded it. Your lawyer pleaded insanity, and you ended up in Radcliffe Asylum again. Your sisters and mother still believe you blew up the bus."

"So it's true that the future always finds a way."

"In a most wicked way. Like I said, nothing changed at all. I met you. We saved lives. Tom Truckle is still who he is, except that he remembers his mission clearer now. The Cheshire came to this world, the Muffin Man was killed, I tricked you into showing me the whereabouts of the keys by pretending to be the Hatter, and we were in Columbia a few weeks back."

"So I really failed in changing anything."

"All but him." The Pillar points his cane at Jack across the street. "He looks happy."

"Yes. He does." I smile. "I am thankful that time let him live."

"*You* let him live, Alice."

"And the Cheshire didn't possess him?"

"No, because they never met. The Cheshire is as vicious as he's always been. Nothing's changed."

"I heard rumors he was dead."

"They're not true. Although he was going to, being left alone in the cold without a soul to posses."

"How did he live then?"

"He possessed a parasite. Some sort of bacteria."

"How convenient."

"He's always been a parasite of souls. He's also the most important Wonderland Monster at the moment."

"Because he knows where Jack hid the keys?"

The Pillar nods, still sharing the view affront. "Pretty stupid move to throw the keys at him in the past, I must say."

"You have no idea how emotionally draining that moment at the bus stations was," I say. "So stop being practical."

"I'd like to sympathize, but if you're going to keep saving lives, you need be stronger than that," he knocks his cane on the floor, once. "But still, you should be proud you saved Jack's life."

"I know, although he'll never talk to me again."

"Yes. That will never happen," the Pillar says. "And it will hurt a lot."

"Sometimes I hate your bluntness."

"Some would argue it's called the truth."

"A painful one," I say. "Any advise how I should live with it."

"Pain is like a glue to the skin. Try to rip it off and it will take a piece of you with it."

"And the solution?"

"The solution is to understand there is no solution."

"That's optimistic." I roll my eyes.

"Once you neglect it will wither away. Pain is like the Cheshire. A parasite. It can only feed on you if you let it."

I have little to contribute to this logic. Maybe because the pain is so fresh. Maybe because I saved Jack, and was hurt again in return. I rest my case."

"And don't worry about the corpse they buried instead of you," The Pillar says. "I took care of things."

I don't even want to know what he did.

"Are we good?" he asks.

"What do you mean?"

"Are you comfortable with resisting the Bad Alice in you?"

"I'm not sure."

"But you're not her now."

I didn't know how to answer that. The concept of having good and evil inside me still makes me uncomfortable. I need time to get used to it and know what I want. "I have a question, Pillar."

"I'll answer if I know. Lie to you if I don't."

"Why am I alive, even though I didn't find my Wonder?"

"Who said you didn't?" The Pillar points at Jack again. "What is a greater Wonder than saving a loved one's life?"

I don't know why I hadn't thought about it. But the Pillar may be right. My Wonder is Jack. Saving his life, to be precise.

I watch him for a bit longer until another girl comes and wraps her arms around him and kisses him. It's my stepsister Lorina.

# Chapter 90

"I guess Jack has a thing for the Wonder family," the Pillar remarks.

I say nothing. Just watch Jack ride his motorcycle with Lorina behind him. I know I have to forget about him forever, although I don't know how. I turn to face the Pillar. "So you did all of this to convert me from a Bad Alice to a Good Alice."

"I wasn't sure it'd work. You made it work."

"And I hated you for pulling me out of the asylum all the time."

"A lot of people hate me lately. I'm familiar with the concept."

"How did you ever know I was the Real Alice?"

"That's a long story. No need to dig up more secrets now. There are more important matters at stake."

"Like what?"

"Like making sure you can control the Bad Alice inside you."

"I don't know if it's possible."

"I guess only time will tell. There are still other important things, anyways."

"Please tell me."

"Another Wonderland Monster is coming."

"This week?"

"Yes. Saying he is the darkest of all is an understatement."

"You always say that."

"This one has a personal grudge against you."

"Really?" I grimace.

"It's going to be a hard test for you."

"Explain, please."

"The next Wonderland Monster is someone you hurt badly when you were the Bad Alice."

"I see."

"He has an agenda of his own. On top of it is making you suffer."

"How will he do that?"

"It will depend on who you choose to be. Good Alice, he will make you suffer by letting you see the world suffer. Bad Alice, he will have to hurt you personally."

"I'm ready for him," I say. There is a certain confidence speaking in me. I feel stronger. Part of me has the cruelty of evil inside. The other part has the innocence of goodness. I believe they can complement each other.

"Ready and optimistic aren't enough reason to face him."

"Then what is?"

"Not being ready. Always be pessimistic in your hopes with a monster. Always believe you will fail. Because if you feel a tinge of optimism, they will see it and stab you the same moment you thought you won."

"I understand," I say. "But seriously, Pillar, why?"

"Why what?"

"Why did you save me?"

"Everyone deserves a second chance."

"That sounds noble, but let's not fool ourselves. I know you're not a saint walking around and doing good deeds. I need to understand why. Please be honest."

The Pillar shrugs. He slowly reaches for something in his chest pocket. He pulls out a yellow piece of paper. It's folded and he grips it hard.

I am curious.

# Chapter 91

"You have what I want?" Margaret asked the Queen of Hearts.

"I do," the Queen said. "But you didn't really have to blackmail me, Duchess. You could just have asked."

"You never listen."

"Then you could just have shut up."

Margaret shrugged. "I need you to fulfill your part of the deal. Give me back what belongs to me."

"I will." The Queen called her guards and told them to let the woman with the red fur in.

Margaret stared at the woman for a long time. It was good to see her, but this wasn't the deal. "Where is he?"

"Patience," the woman in the red fur said, and then clapped her hands.

A chubby young boy entered the room. He licked an ice cream and looked confused.

Margaret's eyes moistened. She opened up her arms, waiting for him to come to her. But the boy stood there licking on his ice cream.

"Don't you remember me?" Margaret said.

The boy shook his head.

"I'm your mother."

"My mother is the woman in the red fur."

"No." Margaret got on her knees. "I am your mother. They lied to you."

"If you're my mother, then you must be deliciously evil. Do you like to hurt people?"

Margaret was shocked.

"Yes, dear Duchess," the Queen of Hearts interrupted. "Your son grew to be one of us. He is a nasty Black Chess member now. I'm proud of him."

"You filthy b—"

"No need for swearing. I took your son from you back then so you'd always do as I say. Now I brought him back. You should be thankful."

"But he is — "

"He is not going to remember you're his mother or return to his old self unless I cure him," the Queen said. "And I won't do that until we win the war."

"So you've planned this from the beginning. You knew you wouldn't give him back to me."

"I may be short, but I'm smarter than you. How many times do I need to spell it out for you?"

"So what do you want from me?"

"To keep working for me, Duchess. Once we win the war, you can have your innocent version of your son back. Until then..."

"The show must go on, I know," Margaret said. "Please don't hurt him until then."

"As long as you obey me."

Margaret hesitated then nodded. "At your service, My Queen."

"Brilliant. We have a new monster coming. A special one. This one has the key to the Pillar and Fabiola's weaknesses."

"Why those two?"

"Because once we find the keys, all we need to win the war is to get rid of those two."

"I see."

"One last thing."

"Yes, My Queen."

"The coming monster never lost a war, so we're expecting someone to die, from us or the Inklings — but it'll be worth it."

"Why?"

"He is one of few who knows how to use the keys."

# Chapter 92

## *The Present: Tom Tower*

"What's on this paper?" I ask the Pillar.

"I wrote my Wonder on it."

"You have a Wonder, like the rest of us?" I chuckle.

"At least, I think it's my Wonder."

"What does your Wonder have to with why you helped me?"

"One day you'll know."

"So you're not showing it to me know?"

"I'd love to, but I'm sensing a few complications on the way. I can't explain much, but let's say I'd like you to keep the note."

"I'd love to."

"Only you have to promise me you'll never open it until I die."

"Whoa. Why are you talking about death now?"

The Pillar steps closer to me. He gives me that look again. "Something strange happened when I was in the future."

"What happened?"

"I went to Carroll's grave to get a stock of Lullaby pills from his corpse."

"You dug him up?" I don't like the sound of that.

"Let's not try to be ideal heroes here. Yes, I dug him up to get the pills and save your life."

I shrug.

"But that's not the point," he says. "On my way out of the cemetery, I came across a tombstone."

"Whose?"

"Someone dear to me was buried there."

"Fabiola?"

"That someone is very important to me. You have no idea how."

"Me?" I say. "But it can't be me. I was alive in the future. My kids expected to see their mum, so I was alive."

"It's not you, Alice," the Pillar says.

"Who is that someone? Do I know him or her?"

The Pillar steps back, locking eyes with me. "That someone is me."

There are no words to describe my shock. No words at all. "But…"

"Don't, Alice," he says. "I'm going before, or some time within the Wonderland Wars"

"Don't say that, Pillar." I step forward. "You will not die. We can do this. We can do this together."

"No, we can't. The future will always find a way."

"But you're wrong. Didn't you see I saved Jack?"

"I think that's why I'm going to die, Alice."

"What do you mean? What does Jack have to do with this?"

"According to the terrible Guide to Wonderlastic Time Travels, time will take a life for every life you save. For every life the time traveller cheats out of time."

I didn't know that. "Are you saying that Jack's life comes at a cost?"

"Yes. At the cost of another life."

"So what? It doesn't say it will be you."

The Pillar shrugs. It's one of the rare moments I've seen him do that. He tries to evade my eyes, but I don't let him, locking on with his. "It has to be me, Alice."

"Pillar?" I tilt my head, realizing I can't lose him now. "What's going on?"

"Time let you save the dearest person to you. In exchange, he will take the next dearest person to you."

And with this I realize the paradox and dilemma. Now that I've learned what the Pillar has done for me, and even though he may have his own agenda, I know he is truly the dearest person to me after Jack.

"Time is vicious," the Pillar says. "I thought I'd live long enough to beat him, but I was wrong."

"Pillar," I say. "No. We'll find a way. We'll…"

"Just don't," the Pillar says. "I'm good to go. Just keep my note. Read it only when I die."

The Pillar starts to walk away. Even now, he is as arrogant as he's always been. He is smiling. Caucus racing, and doesn't give a mushroom about this world. I am out of words — and solutions.

"I think you should look for that future husband of yours," he says, walking away and happily waving his cane in the air. "Get married after you win the Wonderland War, Alice. Have kids. Teach them how to go down the rabbit hole and beat it."

I am standing in place, soaked in my tears.

"But I have a question," he says. "Why name your Tiger and Lily? I thought Lewis and Carol would be neat. But then again, I'm not their father."

The Pillar disappears from view and I stare at the note in my hand. I am staring at the Pillar's Wonder. But I can't open it. I promised. I can't describe how much I love and hate this note. If I keep it closed, the Pillar lives and I never realize his Wonder. I'm afraid if I open it, I will know his Wonder, but he will be dead.

# Chapter 93

## THE PRESENT: PILLAR'S CELL, RADCLIFFE ASYLUM

Tom Truckle, having made a deal with the Pillar, keeps me in the Pillar VIP cell upstairs. It's a lonely place up there in the empty ward. But it's necessary to have everyone else think I'm still dead at this point. I understand.

The Pillar doesn't use the cell anymore. He said he wanted to make something useful out of his days alive. When I asked where he'll be, he said: "Where madness is a virtue."

I can't imagine where that would be, but he promised me he'll have a great time.

All until next week's monster arrives.

Now in the Pillar's cell, Tom brings me my Tiger Lily pot from downstairs. He sets it next to me and asks me if I need anything else. I thank him and he leaves.

I spend hours and hours trying to solve a few mysteries in my head. Like why I had to kill those on the bus, where it was going, and who my future husband really is.

And and why the Pillar really helped me. I keep the note about his Wonder with me all the time, worrying I'll lose it. I need to find a safe place to hide it.

Sometimes Jack comes to mind, but I cry the thoughts away. And then I'm fine.

Even when I can't stop thinking about him, I remind myself he is alive and happy. It helps, not much, but it makes me not cry.

I remember my future husband. I don't know what to think of him. Hey, I'm too young to think of it, even if time pushes me to marry him.

But all I think about are my children. They break my heart. They mend my heart. They make me laugh. Make me cry. I know it's a weird way to put it, but they're the light of my life. They're the reason I will keep on fighting, even though I won't meet them until several years from now.

It puzzles me how time didn't consider them my Wonder. Maybe because they didn't happen yet.

Not that I'm really convinced by the Pillar's explanation of my Wonder, me saving Jack, but I can live with it.

At night, I hug the Tiger Lily pot and think of my children. Then I realize I need to take care of it in a better way. I need to quench its thirst and make sure its roots are fine.

So I spend the night checking the pot.

This is when an idea comes to me. To bury the Pillar's note in the mud in the pot. Carefully, I start digging through it with my thumb.

Instead of tucking the Pillar's note inside, I find another note. One similar to the Pillar's.

What's going on? Did I do this before in the loop of time?

I dig the note up, rub away the dirt, and unfold it. It's in handwriting that I think is mine. The words delight me. They make sense:

This is me, writing a note to me. Don't panic. Time is a loop we'll never understand. Just read the note:

A little lower it says:

You're alive because you found your Wonder. Which isn't Jack. Your Wonder is YOU, Alice. Beating the evil inside.

My heart flutters with a mix of euphoric emotions. I even hug the thin note. I am fine with the Wonder being mine, although I'm oblivious to how and when I wrote this message.

It doesn't matter.

I beat the evil me. I beat my recklessness, my anger, and my weakness to Black Chess. My name is Alice Wonder, and I save lives.

# Epilogue Part One

## St Aldates Street, Oxford

Two days later, I'm discreetly walking near Oxford University. It's heavily raining again. I'm hiding underneath my hood so no one knows I'm alive. My hood is grey, the color of rain. The color of invisibility. In order to make the Bad Alice disappear, the Good One has to vanish as well.

It sucks being invisible. It sucks not having friends. It's been only three days and I feel as lonely as the homeless man on the corner of the Alice Shop I'm passing by.

All I can think about is the Wonderland Monster who is supposed to arrive in a few days. I wonder what I did to him in the past – I wonder what the Bad Alice did to him.

It's almost impossible to keep saving lives, knowing who I really was and how many people I hurt. This isn't so much about doing good anymore. It's more like repenting and giving back to the people I hurt in the past.

What in the world happened to me after the Circus? How did I become a Bad Alice?

I tap my hand on my breast pocket, where I keep the Pillar's note. I really want to know what his Wonder is.

Walking further, I notice a black limousine has been tailing me for a while. I wonder if someone knows I'm still alive. My feet urge me to stop, but it's not like I really want to know who it is. I'm just so goddamn lonely I'd enjoy a conversation with the devil right now.

I stand in silence. The limousine stops. I'm unable to see inside because of its black glass. I wait a little, but no one comes out.

Curious, I step down from the pavement, toward the limo. I reach for the door's handle and pull it open.

The limo is pretty dark inside. But I see silhouettes of people. Silent people.

"Can I help you?" I ask.

"We knew you're alive, Alice," a voice speaks to me from the dark. "But we thought we give you time to heal."

"I'm not sure who you think I am." I say. "Who are you?"

"Let's not play games," the voice says. "How long will you pretend you're not one of us?"

So it's Black Chess. They found me, and they want me back.

I pull back, about to close the door. "I'm not her anymore. She is dead."

"Don't you want to meet him, Alice?" the voice says.

"Meet who?"

"Mr. Jay."

I say nothing.

"Don't you want to know who he is?"

I am not sure what's happening to me. It could be curiosity. It could be my inner Bad Alice wanting to answer to her employer. Her boss. Black Chess. Her past.

I don't know.

"Don't you know if you're mad or not?" The voice says.

I almost flinched at the assumption. I am tired with people trying to mess with my mind. "Is that another Black Chess trick?"

"Not at all," the voice said. "You may have been told we're evil —which is very much a point of view — but the reality is we've never lied to you."

"I won't fall for your this," I stress the words. "I'm Alice Wonder. I'm Mary Ann. I'm the orphan girl. In fact, I'm the Bad Alice. I am not mad."

"You're definitely the Bad Alice. And most of what you just said is true," the voice says. "But not everything you learned is real.

"What do you mean?" My hands grip the edge of the door. An inner urges me to shut it close. Right now, before my heads starts to reel again. I know enough about myself. Maybe it's not wise to know more.

"Come on, Alice," the voice says. "Did you forget about the Lullaby pill?"

"What about it?"

"You've swallowed a whole lot, enough to make you lose your mind."

I should have closed the door. Images of what happened to Tom Truckle hunt me. I've seen him pop the Lullaby pills like M&M's. I've seen what they did to his mind. Who said I haven't been affected like him? I really should have closed the damn.

"The Pillar doesn't have all the answers. Only Mr. Jay, your psychiatrist, the founder of Black Chess, knows the little details about you, Alice," the voice says. "They say the devil is in the detail. In Black Chess, we believe that madness is in the detail."

I'm lost in the space of my head again. What is the person in side the limo talking about? A stranger need overwhelms me. I can't explain it.

"Think about it, Alice," The voice says. "You tried to change the future, and were slightly successful. You saved Jack, but that's all. Everything stayed the same."

"What's your point?" I have a feeling I'm about to get into the limousine. I hate that feeling. But hating something never prevented it from happening.

"The future always finds a way," The voice sounds confident. Comfortable with the darkness it comes from. "We will win the war. It's inevitable, even if you change a few things."

"The Pillar and I will fight you – "

"The Pillar will die soon. That's also inevitable. Give in, Alice. It's fate."

It's hard to explain how I feel in my chest. Those mixed emotions of love and hate. I feel like there is a magnet pulling me inside the limo. I say, "Yes, I want to meet Mr. Jay."

Am I so lonely I want to meet with the mysterious psychiatrist?

"Please get in," the voice said. "Mr. Jay is waiting. He has important plans for you."

And here I stand at the crossroads of my life.

Am I really going to enter Black Chess's headquarters? Will I be a Good Alice and kill them all and save the world? Or will I give into the Bad Alice in me and help destroy the world?

I wonder.

# Epilogue Part Two

## *THE FUTURE: MOUNT CEMETERY, GUILDFORD*

### *THE UNTOLD PART*

When Carter Pillar ran out of the cemetery with the Lullaby pills, his heart raced. He was afraid he'd miss Alice and that she'd die because of him being late. Panting, he was on his way to his motorcycle when something caught his eye.

He suddenly forgot about Alice and approached that something. A tombstone outside the cemetery.

The Pillar stood before it, unable to comprehend what he was looking at. This must have been a mistake. How could this be true? Was this really going to happen?

The Pillar was simply staring at his own grave.

Things didn't get crazier than that. Staring at your burying place in the future while you're still alive in the present.

But that was only half the horror.

It took him a moment, staring at the writing on the tomb. Strangely, there was no date of death. He leaned forward and squinted in the rain.

Something else was written at the bottom of the tomb. A revelation that puzzled him the most. The tomb read:

Carter Chrysalis Cocoon Pillar
Killed by Alice Wonder.

The END...
Alice will return in Checkmate (Insanity 6)

# Thank You

Thank you for purchasing and downloading Wonder. The one book in the series that has very little Lewis Carroll gimmicks, puzzles, or exquisite historical locations. I believe this was necessary in a story about Alice's real past. I didn't want to distract from the feelings and emotions associated with her conflicting circumstances. I wanted you to be involved and as shocked as she is. Add in the complications of time traveling (which I toned down since it's not a Science Fiction book), there was no place for intriguing Alice in Wonderland facts.

If the facts and little tidbits are your thing, you'll love Checkmate (Insanity 6) a lot.

But back to Wonder, which is my favorite book in the series. (I know I say this about each new book, but that's a good sign, because once I feel I can't say that about a book I'm writing, then the next book in the series will be the last.) Wonder is Alice's biggest obstacle. From now on she'll be a larger than life character with a few adult decisions to make. I feel the characters matured enough to create endless conflicts all the way toward the Wonderland Wars – and the very final revelation of course.

Also, I get a lot of emails about the Hatter. He is buried somewhere in a drawer full of researchers I made. He and Tweedledee and Tweedle Dum have a great story to tell soon.

Don't miss the Pinterest page, where you can see all the places and riddles Alice and Pillar visited — and a few images of the Invisible Plague, the Garden in Scotland, and a few other interests. I haven't updated for a while but will on weekly basis from now on. I'm also working on a map of the places she visits.

*You can access it* HERE (Pinterest) or HERE (Instagram)

**Checkmate** (Insanity 6) will be released soon, so please stay tuned to my Facebook Page:

http://Facebook.com/camjace

or

http://cameronjace.com for more information.

If you have a question, please message me on Facebook; I love connecting with all of my readers, because without you, none of this would be possible. http://cameronjace.com

Thank you, for sharing this mad journey with me,

Cam